TRILOGY

THE FREQUENCY

Janja Srečkar

# SKATUR

How far would you go
to discover the truth?

(3rd book)

SKATUR, JANJA SREČKAR

Title of publication: Skatur
Subtitle of publication: How far would you go to discover the truth?
Original title of publication: Skatur
Original subtitle of publication: Kako daleč bi šli, da odkrijete resnico?
Author of publication: Janja Srečkar
Publisher: selfpublishing (Janja Srečkar), Ljubljana
Edition (printed): First edition
Year of printed edition: 2016
Printed by CreateSpace, An Amazon.com Company – Print on demand

Year of first publication (e-book): 2013
Year of copyright protection: 2010
Pictures and ornaments: Pia Rihtarič
Design and layout realisation: www.leparec.si
Translation and editing: Mojca Lorber and Alan Horvatič

---

CIP - Kataložni zapis o publikaciji
Narodna in univerzitetna knjižnica, Ljubljana

821.163.6-312.9

SREČKAR, Janja
    Skatur : how far would you go to discover the truth? / Janja Srečkar ; [pictures and ornaments Pia Rihtarič ; translation Mojca Lorber and Alan Horvatič]. - 1st ed. - Ljubljana : selfpublishing, 2016

Prevod dela: Skatur

ISBN 978-961-94018-2-8

284541184

---

# TABLE OF CONTENTS

*To my mom, my collaborator and my best friend Anka, to my dad Zvone, an unarmed soldier of peace and to my daughter Žana, whose eyes carry the spark of my creativity.*

# Part one

# Zyna

K*AIRON, TURN LEFT!* I quickly shouted in my mind when I saw him getting too close to the big depository. He turned towards me. *How much time do we have?*

*I don't know, but it seems not too much!* I quickly answered.

Transparent coffins containing transparent yellow liquid were stacked one atop another and we were flying as fast as we could.

*Look, over here!* I pointed with my finger. It was as our mentor had said – one of the coffins was actually sticking out of the pile.

We got closer and looked inside. A young boy with black hair, thin lips and somewhat square face was resting in the liquid. In that moment my memory became crystal clear. Above the coffin was an indicator saying:

»Deleted: 95%«.

*Oh, no, we have to hurry up!* I moaned.

Kairon took hold of the coffin's bottom part and grasped a couple of handles. He pulled one out and pushed the other in. The lid opened up and I reached into the liquid with my hand.

The boy had an electrode attached to his head. It was fitted with a needle that was stuck into his brain. I pressed the pin and the electrode opened up. I took the needle out. In that exact moment an even louder alarm sounded. The boy opened his eyes. I handed him a towel, fresh clothes and an oxygen helmet and helped him put on a spacesuit. When he regained full consciousness he started asking questions.

»What happened?«

»There's no time for explanations,« I said quickly. »Come with us if you want to live!«

He quickly climbed on Kairon's hovering platform. Despite both of us driving extremely fast, we weren't sure we would reach the exit in time. We were spotted and the door was beginning to close.

*Faster, Zyna!* Kairon encouraged me. He had to turn his platform upright to get through.

»I'm not losing you,« I said to nobody in particular. »It's still possible to get through!« The door in front of me was almost closed when I pressed the acceleration key even harder…

## I. WHERE FROM?

**»M**om, why am I pinkish-orange and you're green?« I asked her for the fifth time that day. I was incessantly badgering her with questions, but that is supposedly typical for all children when they turn five. Well, at least for the human ones. Orruwin children start asking questions at three. I kept following her constantly and asking her questions.

»Mom, why is my nose in the middle of my head, and yours is in the back of your neck – and why yours looks completely different?«

»Mom, why do you have a tail and I don't?«

»Mom, why is dad yellow and covered with scales? Does that mean that I should be blue, but I got sick later on and turned pink? Mom? How did I come into being?«

My poor mom soon had enough of this type of questioning. She stopped.

»A rocket brought you, sweetie. Like all the other beings on this planet.«

»Where did the rocket come from?«

»Well, from the space.« She pointed her finger at our light-purple atmosphere. »You'll learn about everything else when you turn eighteen. Like other Skaturians.«

»And where… How did…« I tried to connect what I just heard.

»Does space lay eggs? Is space pregnant?«

She looked at me shocked.

»Where did you hear that!?«

»Dad showed me a chip with encyclopedia…«

Mom immediately put down the tray with cookies and headed towards dad's room.

»Xator? Xator? Where are you?« I sensed that she had something important to tell him, so I quietly crawled to the door of the room she went into.

»Yes, honey?«

Mom addressed him with an angry voice and simultaneously tried to whisper, to make sure they wouldn't be heard.

»What have you been looking at with Zyna? Which chips? You know very well that encyclopedias are forbidden until she turns eighteen?!«

»Of course I know, but...«

»You realize that we could get in serious trouble because of that...«

»But honey, calm down...«

»How can I calm down? It's completely unacceptable that she's living so close to her human friend! And now you're going to endanger us too? I thought we were on the same side...«

»Of course we are... She just wanted to know.«

»Not another word from now on. I can't even think about how I'm going to dissuade her from using words like 'laying eggs' and 'pregnancy'. What are we going to tell the city authorities? That she invented everything!?«

Dad became aware of his responsibility.

»Don't worry Tara, I'll talk to her. Nobody will find out about this.«

»You don't need to *talk* to her. We have to forget about all this. Simply forget!«

»OK.«

»I should go before something goes wrong,« she said as she started walking across the room, »I left her alone.«

I quickly backed away and tried to get as far as I could as fast as I could. I wanted her to find me in a position that would clearly indicate that I didn't have my ear pressed against the door just a few seconds ago.

She stormed out of the room and I quickly grabbed one of the warm cookies. I bit into it – to prove that I had been devoting my attention to it the entire time – and praised mom:

»Excellent cookies, mom!«

»All right, sweetie,« she glanced at me, »come and give me a hand with Ska-Line.«

I obediently went after her.

## II. SKA-LINE AND PLANET SKATUR

MY PARENTS WORKED IN A BIG ROUND BUILDING, WHERE IT WAS their job to ensure we were all connected all the time. Every one of us wore a bracelet that was – due to its width – more similar to a forearm armor than a bracelet. All the bracelets were connected through satellites that were constantly orbiting our planet. If we needed anything – information, news, mental state assessment or just to talk to a friend – we used our bracelets. The experts named their connection Ska-Line.

Each bracelet had its color and vibration. Its size would change from year to year. Children had narrower bracelets, while adults had wider ones. The scope of information also changed from year to year. The older the bracelet's owner was, the larger the everyday inflow of information to his Ska-Line bracelet was.

Mom and dad went there every day, and our neighbor Sam would usually join them. He was a hermaphrodite and had a son Kairon, who was the only one resembling me in our vicinity. They would be driven on big moving platforms that enabled sitting. The platform was usually operated by a shining Ska-robot. I liked those beings, even though they acted differently from us: they shined and were always friendly.

The building where the Ska-Line signal was maintained in our neighborhood was really big and mighty. The majority of people in our town – called Nox – worked in it. Ska-robots took care of everything else: food, drink, traffic, clothes…

Planet Skatur was divided into two continents: Left and Right. In between flowed a transparent, hot and toxic liquid we called laza. If we were mischievous, our parents would scare us by telling us we would be pulled in by evil ghosts. Well-protected and guarded bridges led across such streams. Areas where the inhabitants of the planet could see laza with their own eyes were very rare.

Mom often invited me to accompany her to work. I loved that! When she led me through the giant sphere that scanned beings entering the building, my bracelet would shine in gold color and the voice inside the sphere would greet me: »Welcome, Zyna!«

I was always slightly disappointed for having such a small bracelet. The grown-ups would always receive a whole heap of information upon arrival, while the screen on my bracelet would come alive only with shiny animals, like some sort of screensaver.

That building was one of the very few places where I felt truly free! No other place was so spacious, bright and familiar like this one. I yearned for new things, news and ideas, and I had a feeling that I might just find them someday in this giant dome. They were just hiding from me at that moment, but would be mine someday.

Kairon and me often pretended to be generals of the Ska-Line stronghold. We would march up and down the dome and when nobody could see us we pretended to give precise instructions to beings working here what to do and where to go. They were constantly surrounded with Ska-robots that tended to their every need for food or drink.

There was a big laser collector in the middle of the dome. It floated like a big shining ball at the top of the glass ceiling. It collected signals from all the satellites belonging to the Right continent.

*If my bracelet was connected to that collector I could find out absolutely everything*, I'd think from time to time. I had a feeling that there were many mysteries I didn't know about. And which the other inhabitants of the planet didn't want me to find out about. That's why the shining collector seemed so tempting to me.

*Someday I'll be connected with you,* I thought. *Even though I don't know how yet...*

Only the Leaders of the planet had the access to absolutely everything. And I knew that. Even though it seemed impossible, I could feel the whole time that I'd make it someday. Kairon sometimes wanted to touch the shining orb in the middle of the dome with his hand. Yet... he was much too far for that. Besides yearning for information we also shared a lot of other characteristics.

## III. KAIRON

He was my best friend. Since we were the only ones that were similar in appearance, I felt especially relaxed in his company. I couldn't trust anybody as much as I trusted him. That simply wasn't possible.

He had blue eyes and blonde curly hair. I had brown hair and we often compared it. We were the only ones in our town to have hair – and we were immensely proud of it. Nobody else could shake it or have braids done. Just the two of us. Even though my hair was twice as long as Kairon's.

We both had our own personal Ska-robot teachers. Mine was named Naia, while his was Gai. We weren't allowed to be together when we had lessons. Our robots in general weren't pleased to see us playing together. They were constantly looking for ways to keep us apart. Luckily, we had lessons only in the morning and we could be alone in the afternoon.

One day, while we were playing in the yard of our dome – the home where I lived with my parents was completely round – I felt that I wanted to ask him something.

»Kairon?«

»Yes?«

»Do… you remember how we got here?«

»Yes. In the rocket.«

»I know that, but… what about *before* the rocket?«

That question had been plaguing me for some time. I often dreamed images I couldn't connect. In my dreams I saw a dark-haired boy waving at me through the glass casing of the rocket like he wanted to amuse me.

Beside me in the rocket was Karion, also laughing… Suddenly we were engulfed by a bright tunnel…

Karion looked around us. »We mustn't say that, remember?«

»No. What?«

»I don't know exactly myself. All I know is I mustn't remember anything. If anybody asks me anything, I have to say: 'I can't remember anything'.«

I too was familiar with those words.

»But you can tell me if you remember anything…«

»I know I can. But I've been repeating these words for so long that I actually can't remember anything…«

»What about the… dark-haired boy?«

»No.«

»The rocket?«

»No.«

He wasn't too helpful. But I was glad that he remembered at least *something*. I could feel that we were coming from the same source and that was somehow comforting. He was my only connection to the world I felt was a part of me, the world I felt I might even call 'home'…

## IV. POSTS 3 THROUGH 7

I CAME TO THIS PLANET WHEN I WAS THREE YEARS OLD. I immediately got my bracelet, my family and my Ska-robot Naia. For each additional year of my life on Skatur my teacher added new information to my bracelet that I could then access. That made me really looking forward to each new birthday! She'd formally walk up to me and add an additional link to my bracelet, making the object I was wearing around my wrist a bit wider each year.

Because of the importance of the event I would name my each new birthday a 'post'. I can't remember my forth post very well. I do know that my bracelet started emitting a pink glow at that time, but that's all.

The fifth post was an important one, because I started learning the first characters, letters and numbers using my bracelet. Anytime I wanted I'd press the key on the shiny surface and the laser beam that came out of the small screen would create a bigger image in front of me. I'd learn from that image, but there were also a few children from Skatur in it, who had their bracelets turned on at the same time, and I could play with them and talk to them. At that time Naia also started to teach me special movements for relaxing the body and protecting myself against danger. She called them martial arts. She also told me that certain laws of nature applied to my body that I needed to bear in mind. Lizards – for example – couldn't fight in such a way, because they had different bodies. I understood.

The sixth post was even more interesting. Since I already knew how to read I received my first information in the written form. The images and information were more clearly separated. If I wanted to chat I'd press one key, and if I wanted stories I'd press another one. Mom often helped me if I didn't understand something while solving problems or doing calculations. Sometimes she'd turn on her own bracelet so she could help me even more. But every time she did that, she pressed the option 'child present' on the screen, so her bracelet too would show only the information that was suitable for me.

I was also learning about Skatur's animals and waters. In the sixth post I also found out that I was a human. That was supposed to be a special being with two legs and two arms, hair on the head and a heart on the left side of the chest. My mom was a Skaturian schilar. With turquoise-green scales, tail that extends to the ground and glittering excrescences all over the body, this species was considered to be one of the most beautiful and most advanced on this planet.

My dad was a Skaturian lizard. The two species were quite similar, with the exception of his bright yellow color and six extremities instead of four. He can use any one of them for walking – strong muscles enable him to do that. He namely belongs to one of the most powerful species on our planet. His tail is also thicker and more agile.

Kairon's parent was a hermaphrodite. That means that he could have children by himself, but wasn't allowed to.

»Why not?« I asked Naia.

»I can't answer you that yet,« she said quickly. I've always hated that statement the most. Whenever we reached a boundary of what I was allowed to know and what I wasn't, she'd monotonously rattle through the sentence 'I can't answer you that yet'. That was one of the rare things that always reminded me that Naia was just a robot. Kairon never said anything like that to me. He'd always answer me differently. He'd never answer different questions with one and the same sentence. Naia would do that often. And that was seriously getting on my nerves.

The seventh post was, in comparison to the others, a real adventure. Naia invited me to a rocket and presented the entire Right continent to me. It was vast! We needed quite some time to fly across it. It was very symmetrical – like a half of an accurately built sphere. Smaller dots that represented our homes and the bigger ones that were mostly Ska-Line posts, thronged the Right continent like small bubbles.

She also explained that our lives, the life of our planet and, last of all, the existence of Ska-Line depended on the Star that shone its purple light on our planet. Nine moons orbited our planet and when the Star would shine on the Left continent, they would illuminate our side of Skatur.

I also found out that the Left continent was designed for other species and that we weren't allowed to visit it.

» Why not?«

»I can't…«

»… ANSWER YOU THAT YET!« I angrily finished her sentence.

## V. POSTS 8 AND 9

A T THE EIGHT POST NAIA STARTED TO TEACH ME SERIOUSLY. Whenever she noticed that I was too immersed in my thoughts, we went running. Since Ska-robots were similar in structure and limbs to their students, they were able to register students' general state of health and determine the limits of their capabilities. That way Naia was always able to sense how many miles we could run and when I was really tired. At the same time she would always encourage me to explore how I could surpass my physical limits by using my mind.

Naia had also started – alongside the Skaturian, of course – teaching me other languages. She introduced me to the English language. It had a very nice flow and seemed familiar.

»Where does it originate from?« I asked her, even though I could already sense what the answer might be.

»I can't answer you that yet.«

I took a deep breath hoping that the time would come when I wouldn't hear that statement again.

At the ninth post my bracelet was twice as big as it was when I arrived on the planet. I was proud because I also received – in addition to the beautiful fluorescent yellow link – a special laser reader for reading chips that could also be used like a small flashlight. Naia took me to the library for the very first time.

A whole stack of round chips, roughly as big as my palm, was waiting for me there. When I pointed my laser reader at a chip, it began to speak.

Each chip had its own content and there was a sea of them. I was very happy, because I finally got a lot of material to research! I was slightly disappointed though, when I discovered that the vast majority of chips contained stories and fairy tales. I was interested in real information, encyclopedias, I wanted to know who I was and where I came from. Why planet Skatur was full of various beings and where these beings came from.

When I asked Kairon, who I was still spending time with, about these things, he told me that Gai wouldn't tell him anything about that either. Gai was his personal Ska-robot. He too would give Kairon disapproving looks if he noticed Kairon in my company. As if our socializing was actually forbidden. When I was in Kairon's company, I was always slightly apprehensive that Gai or Naia would suddenly appear from somewhere. At the same time it was a pleasant feeling too; it seemed like I was finally able to break the rules in some way.

If Naia couldn't or wouldn't tell me everything I wanted to know and would thus made me angry, I was paying her back by hanging out with Kairon with even greater pleasure. But it wasn't just about that. Kairon was my true friend. He was going through the same changes as I was, he was my size, he ran as fast as I did and he liked eating the same food. I couldn't understand why I shouldn't be with him, when hanging out with him was so pleasant. He even laughed at the same jokes I did. Whenever we quarreled pretty soon one of us would back down from the simple reason: we couldn't live without each other.

For my ninth post he gave me a friendship pendant. It was round and blue. It was encircled by a few light-brown images that were irregularly shaped – some of them were connected. On the top and at the bottom of the pendant there were two white patches, reminding me of white, irregularly shaped corks on each side.

»Wow, that's that? I mean, what does it represent?« I asked him.

»I don't know. I found it in a souvenir store and bought it. When I asked Gai about it, he told me he couldn't…«

»… Answer you that yet. It's all right. I'll wear it with even greater pleasure, then!« I proudly concluded.

I didn't have the faintest idea how seriously forbidden object I got for my birthday. Because the very next day Naia confiscated it.

»WHY?!« I asked furiously.

»You see, that's the problem of your species,« she said calmly. »You get upset so quickly over nothing.« This was the first time that she mentioned me being different from other beings. »That's why it's not good for you to spend time with Kairon. You might not feel that yet, but… With him you'll always be more like your species: always angry and restless. I can't allow that. Not on this planet.«

Even though her answer made no sense at all to me – I was always happier with Kairon, not angrier – I was nevertheless satisfied because at least once in my life I got an explanation that wasn't just simple 'I can't answer you that yet'.

»May I have my pendant back, please?« I tried to say as calmly as possible.

»You'll get it back when you're old enough to wear it.«

And so I lost another one of my rare valuables.

## VI. POSTS 10 THROUGH 14

THE TENTH POST WAS MUCH LESS STRENUOUS. Naia took me once again all over the Right continent. This time she showed me many more beings that lived there. She described regions and their climates to me: everything from the cold northern blue regions to the warm red sandy shores. When we reached the borders of the Right continent, she once again turned the rocket around.

»Are we ever going to fly over there?« I asked slowly.

»No,« she answered, »the inhabitants of the Left and the Right continent are strictly separated. Only the rockets with special permission fly over there.«

I wanted to ask why, but she cut me short. »I'll answer that when you're eighteen.«

Even though I wasn't too pleased with the answer, at least I got a piece of information I could look forward to. I'd obviously get a lot more answers in a few years' time than I did now. All I had to do was wait.

The eleventh post was more interesting because Naia explained in detail for the first time what my body was made of and that I needed oxygen for breathing (my mom, who was a Skaturian schilar, didn't need it). She also explained the changes that were about to occur within me and told me that that was nothing unusual. She showed me the differences between the human male and female.

»Are Karion and me the only humans on Skatur?« I asked her once.

»No. You'll learn more details next year,« she answered.

Maybe that was why my eleventh year seemed to pass by much slower. It dragged by and it just wouldn't end. I counted the days and towards the end also hours and minutes. Finally it was here.

The twelfth post. I called Naia first thing in the morning. She came smiling. She knew I was impatient, although she couldn't understand the feeling. But Kairon could.

She slowly wished me happy birthday and added a new link to my bracelet. I pressed the key immediately. An image appeared on the screen of a man who looked similar to me. His appearance was slightly different: his neck was thicker, his hair thinner and there were a lot more wrinkles on his face. Naia explained that was because he was older. He wore a white coat.

»Welcome to the lecture: 'Who is a human?'!« said the man.

I sat on a chair and made myself comfortable. He mostly talked about things I already knew. But I was glad to hear them for the first time from somebody else. From a real, utterly real man! The only new piece of information for me was mentioned at the very end.

»Humans inhabit the entire planet Skatur. The number of inhabitants of his species is 12,523. There are 6,794 men and 5,729 women.«

I heard the expressions »man« and »woman« for the first time. It seemed amusing that a species would have names for such things. So far we'd always used the expressions male, female and hermaphrodite.

The lecture was over too soon. I had so many questions.

»Next year,« said Naia.

And so I spent my twelfth year too on the lookout for new things to learn. Sometimes Kairon would help me by learning some small detail from Gai. We'd compare information and since it was the same, we concluded it was true. Every new piece of information was more than welcome.

I also noticed that his voice started to crack and deepen slightly. It didn't bother me; it was actually rather nice. Sometimes, when his voice would slightly squeak, he wanted to get away from me. Only when I stopped him and told him that I actually liked that he said in amazement: »Everybody else makes fun of me because of it. Schilars, orruwins and hermaphrodites never squeak. You don't squeak. But I do.«

»But that's completely normal. Naia has talked about that. It happens because you're a *man*,« I said proudly.

»What's that?«

»A human male,« I was even prouder. It was obvious that Kairon hadn't seen the documentary. I asked him about it and he actually got a different link. We found a quiet spot and watched it together.

»Wow,« he was impressed. »Thanks a lot, Zyna. I feel much better now.«

»You're welcome,« I said quickly. »Anytime.«

The fourteenth post was a lot less amusing. The link didn't contain any new information. But it did contain a chip that would come in handy when I turned eighteen.

»That's so far-off,« I said helplessly and tried to learn something more from Naia.

»That won't help you,« she smiled. »That's all for this year. You're definitely the most curious being that ever lived on Skatur!«

# VII. POSTS 15 THROUGH 17

Posts fifteen and sixteen went by quickly and insignificantly. I remember only that I got a few new chips containing information about Skatur.

»They might be more important than it seems,« Naia warned me.

I preferred much more to listen about my own species and to follow the tips where my rocket came from to this planet… I'd been stopped too often by the statement 'I can't answer you that yet'. I'd read and reviewed the entire content of chips and in the end saved them for later. They contained a lot of information – the size of the planet, the sizes of continents, the width of the sea of laza, etc.

The seventeenth post was the most interesting so far. Naia had even allowed Gai and Kairon to join us. She and Gai had namely prepared a special presentation for us, from martial arts to dancing. We learned the traditional dance of Skatur as well as a few dances from other dimensions. They told us that there were five other worlds besides Skatur.

»Galactica, Airon, Lunar, Pteor and… Kanter,« said Naia. She named the last one a bit cautiously.

Gai quickly continued:

»Galactica: a very hot planet. Beings that inhabit it vibrate with exceptional speed. They are very bright and take care of balance in the universe.

Airon: planet, that is rather cold in comparison to Galactica. Ice covers its surface. Since no organic matter can survive such cold conditions the inhabitants of this planet reside in another dimension. They're called the Darkened bacause of their ally, the darkness.

Lunar: planet that connects other worlds with tunnels of light. It's the post and the crossroads for all the mentioned planets.

Pteor is the planet that is most similar to Skatur, with the exception that the population distribution is somewhat different.

And… Kanter. A planet for depositing. Like a depository.«

The last planet awoke a special interest in me. Both Kairon and me were hungry for knowledge anyway.

»Depository? What sort of depository?«

»We can't answer you that yet,« said Naia and Gai as one.

Gai continued.

»As it is customary for all young ones that turn seventeen, we cordially invite you to a special training that will take place in a week's time on the other side of the Right continent…« and when he saw how delighted we were at the thought of joint holidays, he added: »Males and females will be strictly separated in this camp!«

We looked at the floor. I could feel that the robots were especially pleased with that. That's why they didn't mind all of us spending the last few hours together. Because they knew that they would soon separate us again.

A week of preparations went by quickly and soon both Kairon and me were prepared for camping. My mom had prepared for me a few necessary accessories for such a trip and learning in the camp. I received a new link from Naia and mom made a special protector for it, so it wouldn't get damaged outdoors. These protectors were rather stylish and I was extremely grateful for her gift.

She also gave me some waterproof clothes; a pair of glasses that indicated the presence of new beings and vibrated upon detecting a new frequency; and a miniature satellite that could be built into my bracelet, so I could turn it on and automatically find my way home.

Just before our robots put us on different rockets, Kairon whispered to me: »Don't worry, we'll find a way to meet over there!«

This time his strong desire to meet me triggered in me a different sort of pleasure than it had before. My heart started beating faster and I my face felt very hot.

I nervously mumbled: »Yes... gladly.« As I sat in my rocket I started thinking about what he must've thought about my stuttering. That I didn't want to meet him? That I was in a hurry? That he wasn't important to me? Why was I suddenly trembling? Weren't we friends...?

As we departed and he waved to me from his porthole, a thought flashed through my mind. I've seen that before. I've seen him waving at me from the rocket. Only we were much younger then...

We've already experienced so much! Growing up on Skatur, constantly wondering who we were... His squeaky voice becoming much nicer and deeper in the past year. That voice intoxicated me every time I heard it... But *why* was that so!? Why wasn't I intoxicated by the voice of a Skaturian schilar, an orruwin or a hermaphrodite? Why Kairon's voice?

And his scent. In the past year it started to attract me more than ever before. The scent that no other being possessed... Some sort of sweet-and-salty perfume that gently touched my senses every time he hugged me or just stood next to me. When he talked to me a similar sweetness oozed from his mouth and I was always overcome by a desire to draw nearer to his lips and press mine against them... Why? Why his mouth? I didn't think it was just because we belonged to the same species... It was something more. But I couldn't find an explanation for it.

At the same time I was wondering... Did he feel the same way? This heat when I walked by? I'd sometimes look at myself in the mirror and my brown eyes didn't seem as magical as his blue ones... My brown hair jutted in all directions, while his natural wavy hair formed perfect blond curls... My body had developed strange lumps in my chest. His chest was nice, sweet-scented, inviting and flat. It was hard for me to see that he wasn't nervous in my company, like I was in his. He obviously didn't feel the same way. Maybe he liked some other female... Just thinking about that I felt a sharp pain in my chest.

When I was almost on the verge of giving in to my emotions and start shedding tears, Naia woke me up:

»Zyna, get ready, we've arrived!«

I saw that Karion's rocket landed not far from ours and that fact filled me with hope again.

»Don't worry, we'll find a way to meet over there!« was still echoing in my mind as I watched his rocket land. He came to the porthole and waved to me again.

*Does he really care about me? Or does he just want to be my friend? Does he even know that I feel this way? What do I feel!? And what does he feel!?*

Naia brought me back to reality.

»Your things, sleepyhead,« she reminded me and handed me my bag.

I quickly stumbled off the rocket, secretly watching the area where Kairon's rocket landed. Both areas were divided by a fence that didn't seem guarded. I had a feeling that Kairon was thinking the same thing. I decided to call him in the evening.

## VIII. THE CAMP

A s we reached the post I noticed quite a few robots direct-ing their protégés.

First the head of the camp greeted us. She was slightly bigger than the rest of the beings, but she also slightly resembled all of them. Like some sort of a conglomerate of all the inhabitants on the planet. When her skin started to glitter evenly I realized she was a robot.

»Dear females, welcome to the camp for initiation into maturity,« she announced formally. »My name is Xeina and I am the head of this camp. Each day you'll get a special task that you'll have to carry out. You may consult your robot, but in the end you'll have to do it yourselves. While staying in this camp you'll follow the rules that apply here! No outside food or drinks – we've got everything here! No additional chips – you may only use your bracelets that will be inspected first. The equipment is clearly described on the list you received over the Ska-Line. And what's most important: no visits to the male camp!«

That had obviously happened before, otherwise she wouldn't have stressed that so clearly. But it made no difference to me. The big schilar didn't mention anything about calling them and talking to them over Ska-Line.

I couldn't wait for her to finish her speech and point us to our abodes. I was glad that I got a tent for my sixteenth birthday from my mom: I just pressed a button and there was a small dome with a blue light on top standing in front of me. The light served as a lamp, as well as a guiding light to my tent. Each light was of a different color.

When we set up our tents – Naia's was close to mine – our camp looked like a collection of colorful bubbles, which was very nice. I constantly thought about where, when and how I was going to call Kairon. It was more than obvious it wasn't going to happen in my tent: it was too close to Naia's and the robot would hear me with her impeccable hearing.

When Naia laid down to recharge her batteries we said goodnight. I lay in my tent for a while. Then I decided to thoroughly explore the camp. If somebody should ask me something, I'd say I was looking for a toilet.

The camp was divided into three parts: the big and spacious part with tents, where our bubble-like tents with different-colored lights were crowded together; a large dome where our leader resided, with the kitchen and bathrooms; and the biggest part that stretched all the way to the male camp. That part included a forest and was surrounded by a fence. I could see that the tree line was guarded which meant that it would be very difficult to sneak past it unnoticed. Unless I tried at the end of the fence… I also wanted to know which beings served as guards. Robots or some of the other beings? Robots would represent a greater obstacle because they never slept and never got tired. Their hearing and their perception of the world was much better than that of other beings…

As I got past the bathrooms, I hid in the dark and walked towards the first trees extra carefully. I decided to approach the edge of the forest from the side. The other females were crowded around toilets and sinks, so I was hoping nobody would notice if I slipped away for a moment…

I was very happy because my plan seemed to have worked. I reached the first trees and studied the situation. The edge of the forest was guarded by two beings that didn't appear to be robots. The first one was a Skaturian snake, slightly bigger that the rest, and it guarded the area with its head raised up. Maybe that was why its shadow looked almost like an orruwin in the dark.

The second one was a Skaturian schilar. Since the females obviously weren't in the habit of breaking Xeina's rules, it seemed to be pretty bored. The attitude of both guards filled me with hope that I just might remain unnoticed in the dark…

After approximately five more steps I was almost past the boundary. I was looking the guards in their backs, glad that I'd obviously be able to continue on my way without interruptions. Suddenly my bracelet started flashing. It shined like a sun in the darkness. I realized that Kairon was calling me and that I had forgotten to set the bracelet on unnoticeable mode. Both guards turned towards the source of light and started walking in my direction.

»It's going to be an interesting evening after all,« smiled the snake. I froze in fear and waited for punishment.

## IX. CONSEQUENCES

**W**»HAT ARE YOU DOING IN THE MIDDLE OF THE FOREST, YOUNG lady?« the snake stopped me.

»Hmm… looking for… a toilet?« I lied helplessly. It was more than obvious where the toilets were. And where I was.

»Aha. Toilets are over there. I'll escort you,« said the schilar meaningfully.

We walked together to the toilets.

»Thank you so much,« I said courteously. I was hoping that my lie somehow managed to deceive the guards after all.

»Yeah, yeah, you're welcome,« said the schilar and looked at me again. »Listen to me now, little human: we know that you weren't looking for a toilet. You can't go into the woods without Xeina's permission. So, my advice to you is to simply avoid this part of the camp if you don't want any trouble. Understood?«

»Understood,« I uttered scared and snuck into the restroom. When I locked myself in one of the stalls I noticed the bracelet on my left wrist. I was so mad that it betrayed me!

Just as I pulled myself together, it occurred to me: I can send him a message! Here, in the locked stall nobody would notice or hear me!

I immediately started typing.

*Hi, Kairon,*
*I discovered that the only way to your camp leads through the forest*
*where security is pretty tight. Do you have any idea what we could*

*do? I almost got through the first watch when you called and blew my cover!*

*Bye, Zyna.*

I sent the message and decided to wait for a while in the stall just in case. I didn't have to wait long.

*So that was you flashing in the dark? I was ten yards away, on the edge of the fence. I saw two guards taking somebody away and I wondered if that was you…*

*By the way, I'm still here. You can set your bracelet on unnoticeable mode and I promise not to call you again… I found a way to remove some of the material from the fence and I made a hole in it.*

*You're invited to help me widen it. And I can inform you about the position of your guards.*

*Best regards,*

*Kairon.*

Such a quick answer made my heart beat faster again. So, he was so close? And he's still waiting for me? I quickly started typing back.

*I'll do my best. I'll be there in a couple of minutes. I'll call you.*

I decided to try it one more time, no matter what. I had to see him. I quickly unlocked the stall and slowly walked away from the facility. I crept alongside the wall hoping that nobody would notice me. As I found myself in the darkness I quickly typed the message.

*I'm close. How about the guards…?*

*The coast is clear. The snake dozed off and the schilar just bit into its snack. I think you won't have any problems. Try to reach the fence and walk straight ahead.*

*What about the trees?*

*Don't worry, there are just smaller bushes here. Perfect for hiding.*

*How many more steps do I have?*

*Ten more. You've just passed the guards, see?*

*I see, yes. It'd be really good now if I kept as quiet as possible…*

*Indeed, yes. Five more steps. Now stop. Can you see the bushes with green blossoms and large white stamens? I'm behind them.*

I rushed over to the bushes. Behind them was a small space covered with grass and the fence that was slightly damaged on the bottom. The material on the bottom was tattered and spread.

»Do you like it? That's my doing,« boasted Kairon from the other side.

»How are we going to cover this?« I asked feeling happy, surprised and afraid of getting caught at the same time.

»We'll think of something. Give me a hand now,« he said and showed me how to loosen the complex fence construction.

We were faster than I would have thought. The hole was soon big enough for me to crawl through. He helped me and took hold of my hands. He pulled me through and helped me get up.

»Here on our side the woods are less guarded,« he whispered. »I don't know why. Maybe you females are more accustomed to do foolish things!«

I opposed. »That's not true at all. We're just a bit more curious…«

»Well, are you interested in our woods, you curious female?«

»Of course,« I replied lightly when I saw we were moving away from the guards.

## X. FREEDOM

HE TOOK MY HAND IN THE DARK AND I COULD FEEL MY PALM getting sweaty. I was afraid that he would feel it too and found it unpleasant. *Dry palm, dry palm*, I kept repeating to myself as we were walking. I wanted to be as relaxed as possible and at the same time... attractive to him. We arrived at a slightly larger clearing from which we could see three moons in the night sky. A sight that couldn't be seen every night. Suddenly he turned towards me.

»What do you think of it?« he asked breathing heavily, even though we weren't walking that fast. He let go of my hand and I uneasily concluded that my sweating did bother him after all. I quickly wiped my hand on my T-shirt to dry it at least a little. For next time, maybe.

Unfortunately, he noticed that and smiled. »Yes, I know. I'm sorry my hands are so sweaty.«

I was about to explain to him that it was the other way around when he continued: »I don't know why. But lately... I feel so... Eh, forget it, why should I tell you that. You'll just think I'm weird.«

But I couldn't be more interested. »No, no, please, tell me. I really want to know!«

The moons had illuminated his gaze that was piercing me from beneath the golden curls. »Really?«

»Absolutely.«

»Zyna...« he started awkwardly. He sat in the grass and I followed. »Beside you I feel different. My heart is beating strangely and my body is acting differently than before. I've never experienced that before... I look forward to every second I spend in your company, yet I'm somewhat nervous around you all the time. And… I think… I love you.« As he said that I could hear a big relief in his voice. And the expectation of my response, because I was so beside myself I was unable to utter a word. Every single cell in my body was pulsating in expectation.

»Can you say something?« he asked timidly. But I couldn't answer him. My hands reached for his face by themselves and my lips desirably pressed against his.

I could smell his pleasant scent again, which was stronger than usual. Since I was finally able to smell and taste his divine face and the softness of his lips, this taste became even stronger. The intoxication I felt intensified when Kairon got over his initial surprise and started cooperating with me. He slightly spread his lips and we merged in a kiss. He embraced me and lay with me on the grass. We were rolling on the pleasantly cool grass, enjoying the sheer intoxication of the moment. When we managed to calm down a bit, we just lay for a while, staring at the sky.

»Wow,« he said surprised.

»Yes,« I agreed.

»So…«

»Yes, I feel exactly the same as you do,« I explained self-confidently. I felt relieved… I became aware of the insignificance of my previous emotions that burst like soap bubbles. I was happier that ever before.

»What do we do now?« he asked.

»Considering the behavior of Naia and Gai it's probably best if we didn't tell anybody,« I concluded, uncertainly. Even though I wanted to tell it to everybody on the planet!

»But I… I'd like to tell everybody,« he added gently. I could feel he really loved me.

»Me too,« I turned towards him. I drew my face closer to his again and he started to explore it, caress it with his hands and kiss it. I closed my eyes and entirely surrendered to his love.

## XI. FIRST DAY AT THE CAMP

As WE PARTED WITH GREAT DIFFICULTY, WE AGREED TO MEET THE next evening at the same time. It made no difference if we were in our respective tents or not anyway. I couldn't fall asleep the entire night; I could only think of him. As Xeina woke all the females up with her loud bell, informing us that it was morning and that we should get up, I felt strangely awake. Even though I didn't sleep a wink all night, my senses were sharpened in a way and my body soft. Naia noticed that immediately.

»Hey, sleepyhead,« she teased me, »if you're not going to sleep in this camp, you're going to be in a lot of trouble!«

»Why?« I asked, still with my brain switched off.

»You'll soon see why.«

Xeina instructed the robots to distribute breakfast. I'd much more prefer Kairon's company to breakfast. I remembered last night once again and smiled. Oh, how I used to burden myself with insignificant things… And he was doing the same thing. I could feel how this huge void that had been gaping inside me, started to fill. Naia woke me up from my daydreaming.

»Aren't you hungry?« she asked with surprise. »The camp usually makes females hungrier. Well, at least the human ones.«

»Yes, yes, of course I am,« I answered quickly and bit into the sandwich made of soft Skaturian crab's claws.

Immediately after breakfast, Xeina acquainted us with the day's schedule. I was about to practice martial arts with the being of another species, learn imitating various nature's sounds and compete in running.

During the first part of the day I was doing really lousy. My soft body simply couldn't adjust to the exhausting endurance training. Every single being I fought with beat me. When somebody saw that they would fight me, they'd let out a tiresome sigh and usually beat me in a matter of seconds.

»What's wrong with you today?« asked Naia and felt my forehead. »You're not sick…«

… *but in love*, I thought. *And you can't understand that, of course, because you're a robot*, I added joyfully.

Finally the time for a break came, and I ate my lunch with great appetite. Constantly falling to the ground made me hungry. Learning to imitate various animals was very interesting. Our instructor – also a Ska-robot – thought us how to survive in Skaturian wilderness just by imitating predators and their prey.

In the evening, the running competition took place and I came last. I fell behind the others by quite a few laps and our finish times differed by a few minutes. After the competition was over Xeina called me to see her.

»Dear human female,« she said bluntly. »I have to admit that we haven't recorded such poor results in our camp yet. You're very weak for your constitution. Maybe this camp isn't for you. Should I send you home? Or do you think you could put in a little more effort because you want to stay?«

I froze. Send me home – now? Not a chance, I'll fight!

»No, no, I'll be all right, I promise,« I immediately became more interested. I'll sleep more or something. I really wanted to stay here with Kairon.

»You won't recognize me tomorrow, I'll be that fast!«

»Well, see to it that you will,« said the slightly surprised Xeina.

Before I went to sleep I wrote a message to Kairon.

> *Hi darling,*
> *If I want to stay here, I'll have to do much better than I did today.*
> *Since I was thinking about you the whole night, I was the worst in*
> *all competitions and I almost got sent home! I have to get some sleep*
> *tonight. See you tomorrow? Kisses,*
> *Zyna.*

The answer arrived soon.

*So, I'm not the only loser in the camp, he, he? I had some difficulties too. See you tomorrow. And sincerely – I can't wait.*

*Me too.*

*Sleep well.*

*How can I sleep when I didn't get my goodnight kiss?*
*Should I come over there?*

*It's all right. I don't want you expelled for pestering the poor female camp members.*

*One single camp member, actually.*

*It better be just one. Goodnight, darling.*

*Goodnight.*

## XII. LIFE IN THE CAMP

THE NEXT DAY I WOKE UP FEELING REBORN. And in classes I really paid attention and listened. Every move represented a challenge. When my thoughts wanted to wander off somewhere else, I thought of Karion and focused again. I redirected my entire interest, to meet him in the evening, into classes and lessons. Consequently, I soon started defeating my opponents. The hardest fight was the one with a Skaturian lizard, because in addition to its legs it was also able to use its fifth limb – the tail. However, the Ska-robot kept reminding us that everything was in the head. And that really helped. If I was focused on the bright outcome of the fight, such a being represented only a challenge and not fear.

After lunch, I revised the previous days' materials on imitation with pleasure. We also learnt how to climb. It was interesting how differently we undertook this feat – each of us with different limbs. The snakes were the best at it. Closely behind them were iguanas, then orruwin, me and the Skaturian lizard. It was the only time I was better than her. She wasn't very good at climbing.

In the afternoon, we competed in running. Xeina couldn't believe the big change she was witnessing: I came second. The Skaturian schilar was the only one to run faster than me. I also set the record result considering my constitution. No human female had ever run so fast in this camp. When Xeina asked me what had happened to me, I had nothing concrete to tell her. The truth was, I had really strong motivation. I *really* wanted to stay.

I could hardly wait for the evening to come. Unfortunately, I managed to draw a lot of attention to myself with my transformation and I had to make a considerable effort after all the congratulations to sneak off to the toilets and then to the forest past the guards. By the fence – where the hole had remained unnoticed – Karion was already waiting.

»How are you, heroine?« he greeted me.

»I beg your pardon?« I asked surprised.

»We heard today that a miracle had happened in your camp. One of the females started defeating all the others…«

»Oh, it was nothing. I was just strongly motivated not to be thrown out. I'll try to be less conspicuous.«

»It's all right… because I had a similar problem!« he said and kissed me.

And so it went on the entire week. Karion and me studied with pleasure, because we knew what was waiting for us in the evening. Soon he discovered the more private parts of their forest, which we got to know in its entirety pretty quickly. We liked the turquoise green pool of water the most. Water springs were a real rarity on our planet.

We would lie by the water and talked. Kairon hesitated at first, but soon confided in me completely: how he had been observing the changes in his body with uncertainty and how he had nobody to talk to about them, because there simply weren't other people in our town. I agreed with him and we realized that we could have ended all of that much sooner if we hadn't felt so embarrassed. I confessed to him that I'd been afraid of certain things that were supposedly characteristic for women: monthly bleeding and the protrusions on the chest.

»I don't know about the blood… but I like that other thing about you very much,« he said and gently ran his hand down my T-shirt.

I started trembling again and surrendered to his caressing. Soon my entire body ached with desire to surrender to him completely. But it was a sweet sort of ache, which was consuming me from my belly outwards. Everything was accompanied with deep breathing that I also couldn't explain. Kairon was going through the same experience.

Naia also mentioned at my seventeenth post that the time would soon arrive when I would choose a male to raise a family with.

»Have you thought about that?« I asked Kairon on the last evening in the camp.

»Of course,« he answered lightly. »And I've already made up my mind.«

»You have...?«

»You know that. How could I be with anybody else but you?« he smiled. »Would you like to be my mate?« he asked while looking in my eyes.

»Of course! Sure!« I kept answering and kissing him all over his face. I couldn't wait to announce our decision to our parents and our Ska-robots. But we weren't aware of the consequences of our decision...

## XIII. THE MOVE

»MOM, DO YOU REMEMBER THAT RULE THAT I HAVE A YEAR TO decide with whom I want to raise a family?« I said with a smile upon my return.

»Of course I do, honey,« she answered in disbelief and took over the tea tray brought by her Ska-robot.

»Well, I've made up my mind. We both have, actually.«

I noticed the worried look in her eyes. »You have?«

»I've chosen Kairon. Kairon and me have chosen each other.«

What seemed like very good news to me, shocked my mom so much that she dropped the tea tray and everything hit the floor with a loud crash. Although I hadn't seen her cry before, this time she was reduced to tears. Skaturian schilars cry only in the case of death and even then rarely.

»Mom?«

»I knew it, I knew it… How could I let this happen? Where is Kairon? Has he already told his parent…?«

»Yes, of course. Just now.«

»Oh, honey, I'm so sorry. Stupid rules! So what if I'm not allowed to tell you – I'll tell you even if they deport me immediately!«

»Tell me what…?«

»You were supposed to learn this when you turned eighteen. I'll give you at least a hint. You mustn't choose a human. That's not allowed. Skatur is a life-preserving planet for those species that haven't got their own planet. Those species are much too dangerous to be able to live together in harmony. That's why this planet is so heterogeneous. Because the Rulers don't want the history to repeat itself.«

»The Rulers?«

»The inhabitants of the planet Galactica. They take care of the balance in the universe and such was their decision. Your birth planet has been gone for some time now. The humans were simply too aggressive. That's why the Rulers agreed that their opposite race, the Darkened, should disintegrate the planet. It was a sort of recycling...«

This time it was me who was reduced to tears.

»My... planet... doesn't... exist...?«

»No and you'll never see Karion again either!«

»WHAT?« I was completely shocked.

»If he had told Sam what you just told me, Sam is obliged to call the administration. Since you're not allowed to communicate or live together, he'll be transported to the Left continent. That's why that continent exists. Because you can't send any type of signal there. It's impossible.«

I quickly put on my jacket.

»Don't be foolish, child. It's impossible!« she shouted after me. But I didn't care. I ran out and reached Kairon's home in record time. I knocked on the door, but nobody answered. I screamed and walked around the dome to find at least an open window or a hatch. Nothing. Silence. Like Sam had moved away too. I sat in front of the door crushed when I heard a voice in front of me.

»Is this Nox 385?« asked a high-pitched voice. I raised my head and saw a family consisting of an orruwin, a hermaphrodite and a Skaturian turtle.

»Is this the right address?« asked the turtle again.

»Yes, it is. Why?«

They were delighted. »Because this is our new home!«

In their happiness they surely couldn't understand why I ran away crying.

## XIV. THE MESSAGE

WHEN I WAS FAR ENOUGH SOMETHING OCCURRED TO ME: MAYBE everything wasn't lost! If he was sitting in the rocket that was flying above the Right continent, he could still receive my message! I quickly typed the message.

> *Dear Kairon,*
> *If you're still on the flight to the Left continent, please contact me.*
> *You can surely still read this. Please know that I'll do anything to*
> *come to you. We have to fight. Today I've found out a few details*
> *about our planet. I'll surely find a signal and a way to reach you.*
> *If you don't find it first. We've got to make it. Please, help me. And*
> *just so you know: I don't intend to look for another partner. That*
> *wouldn't make any sense. They may as well kill me if they want to.*
> *Answer me, please.*
> *Yours always, Zyna*

Once again I received the answer very quickly. But it was a short one.

> *Dear Zyna,*
> *We can never see each other again. I'm sorry it ended this way. I love…*

After that I didn't hear from him anymore. I wanted to make contact with him, but I couldn't. The connection was cut off. I fell to the ground and cried. He was my true friend. My partner. My boyfriend. My love. My everything. How could I live without him?

After an hour of crying my eyes out I felt the presence of another being. Naia was standing next to me, holding a pendant.

»Since your mother has already told you all the details, I too can transgress a little,« she smiled. »This pendant represents a planet. Your planet. The wiped-out planet. This is planet Earth. This is everything you'll ever find out about it.«

She gave me back my pendant from four years ago. But I didn't want the pendant, all I wanted was Kairon! I wanted him to come back! I held his gift in my hand remembering everything we went through together… I became overcome with emotions again.

»You're not going to solve anything by crying,« she reminded me.

»How do you know!? What do you know about love, what do you know about the feelings human beings can feel!? Nothing! You're just a stupid machine! You've got no idea how I feel! You've got no idea what I'm going through! You've got no idea how it is to love somebody that has been shipped off in cold blood to the other side of the planet! So don't give me any advice I can't understand, is that clear? Leave me alone!«

This was the first time that I actually yelled at her. I ran towards home, although I didn't really want to go there. I turned a corner before I got to the house and sat on the platform that led to the Ska-Line. I wanted answers. Even though I didn't know how to get them.

How do I get to the Left continent? How do I make contact with it? There had to be a solution. Kairon would never write something like that. Maybe it wasn't him who wrote that after all. Or maybe it was dictated to him. He wouldn't reconcile himself to the fact that we weren't to see each other again. I knew he wouldn't.

When I got there, I burst into the building. Near the top of the dome I noticed – like so many times before – a shining orb, the data collector for the entire planet Skatur.

I stared at it, trying to think of a way to get to the data…

## XV. CRIMINAL OFFENCE

WHILE WATCHING THE GLIMMERING DOTS GLOWING INSIDE THE big orb I remembered that I had a chip-reading laser in my bracelet. Could it also read the data from the collector? Could it be that simple? Even though my idea was undoubtedly illegal, I decided to carry it out. I set my bracelet to the unnoticeable signal. Even though the building had a very tight security, I was hoping to go unnoticed in the crowd.

I turned on the laser and started directing it. I was aiming directly at the center of the orb. And I hit it. The screen said:

*Entering system center. Continue?*

I typed in: *Yes.*

Soon a new communication appeared.

*Access permitted only to the supreme authorities of the Right continent of planet Skatur. Choose your identity.*

I thought it would probably suffice if I entered the name of the Leader of our town Nox.

*Gnosis Dral.*

A new communication.

*Hello, Gnosis Dral. Your password?*

Damn, I hadn't thought of that. I concentrated on what was so important to our Leader that he would choose it for a password. He had a daughter named Kaia and a wife named Ika. And a tiger named Gauli. I decided to try them one by one.

*K-a-i-a*

And *enter*.

*Welcome, Mr. Gnosis*, it said on my bracelet.

*I can't believe it, I'm in!* I thought ecstatically and my hand began shaking. *Now I have to make good use of every second!*

I quickly started entering search terms.

/Left continent/ /Kairon Katir/ – /Sam Katir/ /Area?/

The map of the Left continent appeared in front of my eyes for the first time in my life. It was pretty similar to the Right continent, with slightly bigger percentage of water areas. A flashing arrow appeared on the southeastern side.

I clicked on it. *Enlarge*.

I kept zooming in until the address appeared.

Hax 231. When I zoomed in even closer, a round house appeared on the screen with a rocket parked next to it. So they'd just arrived! My eyes filled with tears when I caught sight of Kairon again, because I was certain I'd never see him again.

He was very unhappy and there were big dark circles under his eyes. I could see from afar that he had been crying. Gai was trying to escort him into the building, but Kairon violently pushed him away, pointed a finger at him and started shouting angrily at him. Since it was a satellite transmission without a sound, I couldn't hear what he was saying. But it looked pretty similar to what I had said to Naia earlier.

*If you knew, my darling, that I can see you*, I thought, *you surely wouldn't be in such a bad mood. I'm coming.*

As Kairon ran into the house and I feverishly searched for a possibility to follow him via satellite, I felt a hand on my shoulder. I froze.

»What are you doing, miss!?« I heard the strict voice of the guarding Ska-robot.

## XVI. THE SENTENCE

B<small>EFORE</small> I <small>COULD ANSWER HIM HE SEIZED MY ARM WITH THE BRACELET.</small> He immediately found out what I had been doing. He firmly took me by my shoulders.

»Please, come with me.«

*Like I have a choice*, I thought as I walked in his iron-firm grip.

When we got to the elevator he turned me away from the control panel. He pressed a few buttons and the elevator started descending. The descend lasted forever. Occasionally I had a feeling that the elevator wasn't moving just downwards; I could also sense left and right turns. It finally stopped after ten minutes. The door opened and we found ourselves in a tightly guarded room. There were armed Ska-robots all around us.

The guard took me to the reception office and said:

»Juvenile delinquent.«

»Room 231,« said the schilar behind the desk.

He wasn't any gentler as he led me to the mentioned room. He knocked on the door and when we got the permission, we went in. Naia was waiting there.

She immediately came to me.

»What have you done, Zyna? Don't you know that's a serious offense? Beings get sent to prison for that, or worse…«

»What could be worse than prison?« I asked in disbelief.

»You better hope that you never find out,« she answered. I didn't care about any of this – had they decided to lock me up, I'd have found a way to escape. The important thing was that I knew the address: Hax 231. And the house – I remembered exactly what it looked like. I wasn't worried about what they'd do to me. I only felt sorry for Naia – she was responsible for me and my proper behavior until I turned eighteen.

A Skaturian schilar entered the room and I had a feeling that she outranked all the others. I was right; she was a judge.

»What have we here?« she asked while I was being seated in my chair. She took the chip and pointed her laser at it. As she watched the incident on her screen her face reflected disbelief.

»Breaking into the database? Under our Leader's name? How dare you, young lady?« Although she represented justice and authority she couldn't help herself from getting upset by such a serious offense.

»I'm sorry,« I uttered quietly.

»It makes no difference to me whether you're sorry or not,« she quickly answered. »The sentence will be the usual one: lifetime…«

»Please, your honor, Zyna is just a child!« Naia interrupted her. She had truly been programmed to protect me. Even from the trouble I got myself into…

»She's what?«

»I mean, she's still underage,« Naia corrected herself.

»And in one year she won't be anymore,« insisted the judge. It was funny watching them argue about my future and not being able to do anything about it. So I decided to keep quiet… What should I have said? »The entire system on this planet is wrong«? »I want to be with Kairon«? Who'd be on my side?

»And if she repeats such an offense in a year's time, you can sentence her like any other adult being on this planet. But before that – if you agree – show her clemency,« respectfully concluded Naia.

»Well, let's see what we should do with you, delinquent,« said the judge again. She started reviewing the data on her screen again. Her face became awash with outrage again.

»And the use of the intercontinental satellite!«

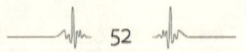

»She's still underage,« persisted Naia.

»All right,« said the judge after a long deliberation. »You'll receive a sentence for the underage. Your punishment will be most severe, so you'll remember not to do such things in the future,« she seemingly reprimanded me, although I could feel that she'd have gladly given me a double or triple punishment for the offense of such proportions.

»Confiscation of the bracelet and deletion of the last month's memory.«

I couldn't stand that. I stood up and shouted out loudly.

»NO! Please don't do that!«

The judge was pleased that she managed to step on my toes.

»And why not? What you've done is against the law, therefore you have to atone for it.«

I could see that she didn't have the slightest idea what a devastating loss that would be for me. She'd delete the best part of my miserable existence here. I couldn't let that happen.

»Please, don't! Please have mercy on me! You don't know what that might do... mercy, please!«

I desperately looked at Naia, who had been rendered totally speechless. I collapsed on the chair and burst into tears. After the verdict a couple of Ska-robots took me out of the courtroom. I helplessly looked at Naia, who said: »Don't worry, I'll let your parents know.«

Soon I lost sight of the courtroom and the robots took me to some sort of a hospital room. But I didn't give in. I wasn't going to let them interfere with my relationship with Kairon. I had managed to break into the orb's database and now they were going to delete my most precious memories: of Kairon and my home. Everything my mom had told me about planet Earth...

The robots placed me on the bed and strapped my body down with special steel straps. I couldn't move at all. I kept repeating in my mind: Hax 231, Hax 231, Left continent, Kairon, Kairon...

They took away my bracelet without any effort.

»Don't worry, you'll get another one,« said the first robot, »only with that one you won't be able to cause any more harm to planet Skatur.«

»What about my memory? Please, delete one hour, one day. But not the whole month!«

»Instructions are instructions,« said the robot. I knew I wouldn't be able to persuade him with anything. I lay there totally helpless, watching him prepare the injection for me.

»Please, don't do this,« I whispered as he approached me. *Hax 231, Hax 231, Hax 231.*

I felt a little sting as the needle broke a hole in my skin. *Hax 231, Hax 231, Hax 231...*

I fell asleep repeating the same phrase.

## XVII. DREAMS AND REALITY

»QUICKLY, THERE'S NO TIME FOR GAMES,« *SAYS A BLACK-HAIRED BOY TO US. He fastens our seat belts. I feel something's not right, but I don't know what. I miss my mom.*

*»Where are you going, uncle Derek and where's mom?« I ask him.*

*»Everything's fine, kid,« he answers, »you're going on a short trip...«*

*Kairon, who is waiting in the capsule next to mine, asks: »Can I go too?«*

*The boy laughs, but I still feel something's wrong. »You too, but right now you have to be completely quiet!«*

*»Later you can talk through this,« he says and shows us a silver button. It's nice and shiny...*

*»Are you ready?« he asks us smiling. I like to play. And I like magical trips. »Yeees,« we reply enthusiastically. I notice that his eyes are full of water.*

*»Is everything all right, uncle Derek?« I ask.*

*»Yes, it is. Something's got in my eye. Listen now. You're going on a magical trip and you have to promise me something. When you land, the world will be full of fairy-tale beings of all sorts and colors. But you have to remember something: if anybody asks you where you're from, you have to say that you don't remember anything, all right? That's very important!«*

*»But uncle Derek...« Kairon protests.*

*»If you don't do that, those beings will hide me so well that you'll never find me again,« says uncle, like he is telling us an exciting fairy tale. »You'd like to see me again, wouldn't you?«*

*»Of course, uncle,« I confirm.*

»Well, all right. Here you go…« He kisses us and closes the glass lids.

»See you,« he waves at us. As we take off, we start pressing the silver button and we talk. Then we notice a few dark shadows that shoot past us. Soon we look back and the trip isn't so magical anymore. The blue planet is disappearing! Mom, where is mom?

I start to cry at the top of my voice and so does Kairon…

»Mom, where are you!? Where's dad!?«

I woke up and realized I was completely covered in sweat. As I wanted to get up I noticed mom standing by the bed.

»Mom? What is it?« I asked when I noticed a worried look on her face.

»Ah, it's nothing, sweetie, you've had a nightmare,« she explained. »Get dressed and come to breakfast.«

I slowly got dressed. I felt sad somehow, but I didn't know why.

I'd been dreaming about Kairon, with whom I haven't talked for quite some time. *Where is he?*

I tried to remember when I last saw him… A month ago? He had obviously distanced himself from me… I didn't know how to explain the way I was feeling… I felt like the previous month had rolled by in a dream I desperately tried to remember, but knew in advance that I wouldn't… One single word resurfaced.

Hax.

What was that about…?

I wrote it in my bracelet – which was also pretty different than before – and went to breakfast.

## XVIII. THE CONTACT

THE DAYS THAT FOLLOWED WERE ALL ALIKE. I felt no excitement, had no wishes, displayed no feelings… I was completely numb. Naia visited me every day – like she always had – and we continued our studies. I wasn't doing very well. Sometimes even she thought that was strange. It was like teaching a parrot. I'd mechanically repeat some things after her and I'd forget the others as soon as she'd utter them. It was the same with physical education and martial arts. I was interested in absolutely nothing.

It was completely the opposite when I went to bed. When I fell asleep I'd often dream unrelated images of the camp, Kairon, the big orb in the center of the dome and a mysterious brown-haired woman and I felt infinitely sad. I often woke up screaming. When I was awake, I couldn't remember anything. Only the numb sensation of repressed mourning reminded me that I'd experienced something important in my dreams.

After a month of such existence – I still couldn't remember anything but the word Hax – something changed. When I closed my eyes I'd get a feeling that I wasn't alone. In my numbness, I'd ignore that feeling and try to sleep.

*Hello, Zyna*, I heard a voice in my mind.

I jumped out of the bed. »Is someone here?« I turned on the light.

*Yes and no. I communicate with you through thoughts. Today I'd like you to be awake when I talk to you.*

I checked if I was awake. Indeed, I was *very* awake. Nobody had ever made contact with me in this way. Inside my mind, inside my head. It was slightly unpleasant – like somebody wanted to talk to me inside a very intimate space, that I'd had only to myself until then. Like inside the toilet stall. I heard soft laughter.

*This feeling will soon disappear and you'll get used to me.*

I realized that this being, obviously a female, could read my thoughts and that it didn't matter if I spoke or not. So I simply thought of the next question.

*Who are you?*

*We're related, in a way. But that's not important at the moment. If I tell you who I am, you'll experience a rush of emotions and we don't want that. I don't want them to drug you up again…*

*What was that?*

*You don't remember that, of course. But you're certainly well aware of the fact that you're waking up all sweaty every morning, trying to connect the events you're dreaming about but can't remember; something is bothering you, but you don't know what. The only thing driving you forward is a strong sense of sadness telling you that something was real…*

*How do you know all this?*

*It's my job to know. Do you want to know too?*

*Of course.*

*But you have to promise me something first.*

*What's that?*

*That – after I've shown you who you are – you won't go berserk like a wild animal. That's why I've waited so long for you to get used to your apathy. Because they'll drug you up again if you succumb to the feelings of anger and resentment. Do you promise to remain calm?*

*All right. I promise.*

*I'll reveal my presence to you now. Please remain calm.*

Suddenly I noticed a white cloak in the corner of the room that wasn't there before. Like somebody conjured it up. I realized it was a hooded figure. As she took the hood off, she revealed her straight brown shoulder-length hair and her indefinably young face. She was undeniably a human, even though she acted differently than me. She was much calmer and sort of cheerful. Deeply happy.

I was stunned because I'd never met such a being before. Her lips were full and constantly slightly smiling. As if she knew the truth of the entire universe. Her eyelashes were nicely shaped and long, with a pair of eternal eyes glittering under them. I could easily compare her to the beings from the book of legends and fairy tales Naia gave me for my ninth birthday. Like somebody created a perfect being. A perfect human being.

*We don't have the time for such superlatives at the moment, but thank you anyway*, she smiled.

I'd forgotten that she could read thoughts, which was still slightly surprising.

*Come here, to the center of the room and sit on the floor like me.*

She crossed her legs and sat down. I did the same.

*Relax*, she said, *and close your eyes.*

I closed my eyes. After about a minute of relaxation I felt my body being relaxed even more than when I was asleep. It was heavy in a way, but my soul was light. I could feel that my body and my soul were pretty different… And then something extraordinary happened. It felt like somebody put a conducting electrical device exactly in the middle of my forehead. An enormous quantity of light surged through me and I had no choice but surrender to it…

This light soon filled my head and spread through my entire body… Suddenly I felt like my body had been benumbed all along and I wasn't able to manage it like I wanted. Like when a part of your body 'falls asleep'. Only in my case my entire body and my soul had been asleep at the same time. Only the sadness that I couldn't explain remained.

Now even this sadness withdrew and gave way to the memories that started flashing to the surface with the speed of lightning:

WHY HIM OF ALL PEOPLE? His scent… Why do I feel like that when I'm with him? Does he feel the same? The camp… »I've never experienced that before… I think I love you.«… »But I'd like to tell everybody…« The decision… »I've chosen Kairon. Kairon and me have chosen each other.« Her worried face… »You'll never see him again!« His departure. The messages. The orb and the laser. Hax 231. Their round house. Kairon pushes the robot away and runs into the house. »What are you doing, miss?« The sentence. The injection.

Then a new scene followed and I was able to see myself through somebody else's eyes. I was still lying on the bed and a couple of skilful Ska-robots were standing beside me. They were obviously doctors.

»THE DRUG KANTAR?«
    »Yes.«
»Separation from emotions too?«
    »Yes, of course. Something like that mustn't happen again!«
    »All right.«
    The other Ska-robot took some vials and started preparing a mixture. When he was finished he injected it into my vein. I moaned even though I was asleep.
    »Such a strong attachment,« concluded the first one with surprise. »Nobody has reacted like this so far. The record, please.«
    The assistant Ska-robot handed him the record. The doctor wrote in it: »Particularly dangerous subject. Strict supervision and observation.«
    Then they left the room. After a while my parents entered the room accompanied by Naia.
»I did what I could,« she said calmly.
    »It's all right, Naia, it's not your fault,« said mom.
    »At least now she'll finally stop asking where she is from and what

her planet is like,« concluded dad.

An interesting question formed in my consciousness.

*Why aren't they interested in knowing where they come from? Why doesn't anybody else on this planet want to know why we're so different and why the rules of living are as they are?*

*Good thinking,* answered my cloaked visitor. *Take a closer look at the serum the doctors injected in your vein...*

I took a look. The bluish-green serum that was coursing through my sleeping body had a special frequency. Since I already felt like I was dreaming, it didn't seem so unusual to be able to see through bodies. I could see the vibrations of things and people. I noticed a similar serum in the blood of my parents.

*Everybody... is injected with... the drug?* I asked surprised.

She nodded. *Everybody except you and Kairon.*

*What kind of a planet is this?* I asked horrified. *And how is that the two of us don't have the drug?*

*The time will come for such answers,* she said. *The important thing is that you know who you are.*

She brought her left hand close to my forehead again and took me back to my room with a beam of light. I quickly opened my eyes and gasped for air.

There was nobody in the room but me.

»Hello? Miss?« I looked around. I couldn't see her or her white cloak anywhere. But I did have my memory. And my body. I had a strong sense of peace and happiness. I knew who I was once again. I entered all the data that I'd remembered into my bracelet. I wasn't taking any chances of losing it again. Happy and deeply reassured I went to bed. Before I drifted off to sleep I gently thought:

*I didn't have the strength, Kairon. It'll be different now. I'm coming.*

# XIX. THE GAME

THE NEXT MORNING I WOKE UP WITHOUT MAKING A SOUND. I simply opened my eyes and felt the lightness in my head. I felt completely refreshed and fit. There was no trace of sadness and my heart was beating in its own rhythm once again. I remembered absolutely everything I witnessed during the night and I was infinitely grateful to the brown-haired visitor, whoever she might have been.

Mom came into my room. I remembered in what I had learnt about her the day before and I finally understood why we were so different. Why we all were so different. And why I'd felt so lonely my whole life. Why I could talk truly freely only to Kairon – without feeling the glass wall between us.

Now I understood her having been drugged for a month myself. I had no idea how it was possible that the effects of the drug seemed to have evaporated almost overnight. I also remembered the advice not to attract attention to myself. If I should feel good and happy it'd be good to keep that to myself. The same rule should be observed if I felt angry. After all, my medical record said: particularly dangerous subject, strict supervision and observation.

I decided to try to act as I did a day ago. I calmly looked at her and tried to make my facial expression as apathetic as possible. A bit too much, as it turned out, because she asked me slightly worried:

»Are you all right?«

»Of course,« I smiled lightly.

»Yesterday you went… to your room pretty early.«

»I told you I was going to bed.«

»I know, I know. But… it seemed to me that you didn't go to bed straight away. I heard voices coming out of your room.«

Did she have an ear pressed against my door or what? Was she a part of the »Strict supervision and observation« project?

»No, I was just singing a song,« I quickly tried to come up with an excuse.

»Well, all right,« she said and invited me to a breakfast.

»I'll be there right away,« I called out after her.

As I was getting dressed I heard a familiar voice again.

*Go on with getting dressed, Zyna. Please act like you don't hear me. You should know your room is equipped with cameras.*

*What?* I thought while I started to sing a random song I supposedly sang the day before.

*I forgot to mention that. But don't worry. You were the only one who saw me. But you'll have to be more careful about everything you do. No more entering data in the bracelet. Delete everything you have in there. And try to act as normal as possible.*

*I'm trying!*

*Be more convincing because your mom doesn't really believe you.*

*Impossible,* I thought. *Strict supervision and observation… Is it possible that I live on such a planet!?*

*Control your emotions, Zyna, otherwise we won't get far.*

*Well, all right.*

*Go to breakfast. Then, when the time is right, I'll contact you again… Bon appetite. And stay away from the beverages in the kitchen!*

And she was gone again. I quickly erased everything I entered into the bracelet. The way things were going at that moment I knew I'd have to remember everything! I was reassured and grateful. Even though I didn't know my future or what lay ahead. But I knew one thing: finally I was back in the game. And this time I had a mighty ally!

## XX. THE TEACHER

IT WAS QUITE DIFFICULT TO EXPLAIN WHY I WASN'T THIRSTY DURING the breakfast – I also had to be perfectly calm and even slightly apathetic. After that I was permitted to go and see Naia. When we were studying I was slightly more interested in the subject matter than usual.

»We're progressing!« she was satisfied. And I just wanted the lesson to be over as soon as possible.

After the lesson I'd usually go home. This time I turned towards her.

»Naia?« I said.

»Yes?«

»May I please go for a walk for an hour or so? Could you let my parents know?« I asked calmly.

»Of course,« she said, not showing any signs of suspicion. Maybe robots were less sensitive in this respect.

*That's true*, I heard the familiar voice. *Go on.*

»Thank you so much,« I added convincingly. »See you tonight!«

*Excellent. Now slowly walk to the main square.*

*What are we going to do there?*

*You'll see.*

I slowly walked to the square. In the middle of it was a statue of our Leader Gnosis Dral.

*Excellent. Here is the biggest concentration of beings, which means that due to the large number of bracelets and different signals yours is the hardest one to catch. Go to the statue.*

I did as she told me and saw a little door at the bottom of it.

*Pretend you didn't notice it! Go around the statue! Quickly!*

I quickly turned around and circled the statue once more.

*When I give you the sign, go to that door.*

*How do you know all this?* I was surprised.

*You'll soon find out. For now just wait nearby. Go to the inscription and study it.*

I went to the inscription at the base of the statue and pretended to read Dral's biography.

*When I say »go«,* I heard her voice.

*Ready, steady, go!*

A couple of schilars comparing the colors of their dresses rushed by me. I quickly stepped to the door, opened it, slipped through it and closed it behind me. In front of me stood my last night's visitor. She stepped to the door and additionally bolted it.

*Nice, isn't it?* she thought.

*Are we going to talk this way here too?*

*We have no choice. We can't afford to be heard in the middle of the square. At the same time, this is the safest place in the city for practice. And, ironically, the most dangerous.*

The room was big enough for relaxation, and I could practice some karate moves if I was careful. A small lamp hung from the ceiling, indicating that this hidden room had been in use for some time.

*This room is intended for secret meetings of your planet's Leaders. There are several such points around here. This one is the third in your city and the closest one to your home. Since it's intended for privacy, it's one of the rare places that doesn't have any cameras or satellites. At the same time it's – as I've already mentioned – surrounded with disruptive signals, so nobody that sneaks into it can be detected. But you have to find the right moment to approach the door. There are ten rotating cameras placed around the entire square. You have to seize the moment when none of the cameras cover Gnosis Dral's statue.*

*Ten cameras? How did you know...*

*I'll explain that later. Soon you'll know how to calculate the right moment without my help.*

*If this room is intended for secret meetings, how do we know we won't be disturbed? I mean, how do we know there isn't going to be a meeting while we're in here…?*

*I like this question better. We just know – by feeling. Besides, the Leaders never meet during the day, because they'd be absent from their duties. And they can't afford that. I'll also teach you how to recognize their schedule regardless of the time of day.*

I was completely overwhelmed. Not only had I an ally, but I'd obviously learn about things I thought impossible until now.

*But,* I thought, *we don't have much time. I told Naia I'd be home in an hour.*

*All right, you'll be home in an hour.*

*But how will I study, if I only have an hour each day at my disposal?* I asked eagerly. I'd rather spend my days and nights there.

*Soon you'll discover that we can bypass certain rules. Your appointments with the Ska-robot, for example. You'll realize that robots are not as invincible as they seem. And Naia could be of great assistance to us if we use her properly. She could even come with you…*

*What? With me? In here? So she can get all this information?*

*You don't understand. When you are strong enough, you'll be able to control her and not the other way around… Only one question remains.*

*And that is?* I asked.

She looked me in the eyes. *Do you want me to teach you? Do you really want that?* she emphasized.

After everything I just heard I felt the cells in my body charging like a battery that had been completely flat. I urgently needed that knowledge, I'd always needed it. I was willing to die for it.

*Of course I do,* I thought eagerly.

*All right. I can see you're telling the truth,* she thought with satisfaction. *If you want me to teach you, you have to know who I am. My name is Timeless,* she said and offered me her hand, *and I'm one of the rare beings that have survived and are connected with you.*

*How…*

*That's enough for now. Go now,* she added attentively, *the time is up. See you tomorrow.*

# XXI. MY FIRST LESSONS

I N THE FOLLOWING WEEK I WAS EXPERIENCING A REAL REBIRTH. At home it was harder and harder to fake apathy and disinterest for life when the knowledge, I had been longing for so long, had finally found me! The universe was opening up in front of me and I was absorbing Timeless' knowledge like a sponge...

*It's important to be aware that you – as long as you exist in this form – depend on your body a great deal. It's like driving a vehicle that has its own set of rules: ignition, brakes, gas pedal... All that isn't you, you're just the driver of the vehicle.*

*What do you mean by that?* I asked eagerly.

*Your body is like a vehicle – built of different parts that can function well or less well. The fact that you're feeling a certain unpleasant emotion is simply a sign that one of your organs isn't functioning well, nothing more. It's vital that you're aware of the following correlations: kidneys – fear, liver – anger, spleen – thinking, lungs – resentment, heart – confusion.*

I was surprised. I'd never thought about my body in this way. I'd thought that *I* was the one feeling the emotions, not my body.

*All members of your species had thought that,* smiled Timeless. *They'd thought that they were what they experienced. That's why they persevered in agony until their planet was doomed.*

*Is it really possible that somebody persists so long?*

*If they don't have the knowledge, then it is.*

And so I learned to see my emotions in a much more technical sense, like defects in the vehicle. That was extremely helpful, especially when I was attacked by doubtful thoughts about Kairon, or thoughts of control I was subjected to, or the pressure I was under knowing all the time how little time we actually had.

Whenever I felt the fear of being caught and put once more in the room with injections, I thought about how my kidneys still must be weak. Like I needed to change a spare part or a program in my vehicle. Such thinking immediately improved my mood and filled me with a pleasant feeling of determination. I wasn't my body – I was just the one managing it. And my body would follow me, no matter what.

This way I also had a much better control over myself. I fought better, ran faster and was able to quiet my mind easier. I studied more intensively because I knew I had to remove my thoughts and prepare my mind for new knowledge.

Everything was happening much faster than ever before. Like somebody had suddenly torn apart the bonds that had confined me all those years and attached me to a rocket rushing towards the goal. Timeless illustrated each of her statements with practical examples. When we were relaxing I really had to follow her instructions. Since she could read my thoughts, I couldn't just ignore her and think of something else, like kissing Kairon, for example.

*It's important for you to live this, to do this seriously*, she reprimanded me. *How are you going to save him, if you just think about him…? If you just philosophize and talk about him? How are you going to acquire new abilities, if you just talk about them? You have to work on it. Really work. Every day. Every second. Monitor your thoughts. Make your being a highly guarded alarm system. Be on the lookout the entire time: »Am I really implementing the knowledge I've been learning? Or am I just thinking about it?«*

I have to admit that at first it really wasn't easy to do what she instructed me to do. When I succeeded, it went fast, but sometimes I couldn't see a few inches in front of me. That was especially obvious a week later, when Naia mentioned Kairon after a long time.

## XXII. A MISTAKE

»COME ON, LET'S GO RUNNING,« SHE SAID AS SHE USUALLY DID WHEN we were finished with the lessons for the day.

I loved running even though I sometimes got a pain in my side. Naia had taught me a long time ago that that was simply a sign that my body was getting stronger and my overall fitness was improving. During the run as well as during the day I'd usually think of Timeless quite often. It felt nice to have a confidant on this planet of oblivion!

At the same time she wouldn't tolerate my ego for a second. She simply wouldn't put up with any kind of pampering. The training was very strict; in truth, we didn't have the time for anything else. We had a chance of beating the time only if we applied military discipline. We had less than a year until Kairon's eighteenth birthday. We could still make our escape within that time frame. After the coming-of-age ritual such a feat would be much less feasible.

»What are you thinking about, sleepyhead?« Naia interrupted my thoughts. I was glad that she still didn't suspect anything, even though I had been going on my »walks« for about a week now. These walks were getting longer by the day, sometimes lasting for hours. Naia always managed to neatly explain away the facts to my parents.

I decided to inquire what she could tell me about Kairon. I'd have to pretend to be apathetic, of course.

»Kairon, actually.«

»What exactly about him?«

I paused a little to form the most careless sentence I could come up with. »He's been gone a long time, don't you think?«

»Of course he has, they have moved away.«

»Really? I didn't know that,« I lied. Strictly speaking, nobody's told me that since I've woken up.

»Well, we didn't want to burden you with that,« she explained. »Sam and he left.«

»Where to?« I asked unaffected.

Naia waved her hand. »What do I know. That's not important anymore. You'll never see him again.«

Even though I knew these words weren't true, their vibration burned me all over the body.

*What do you know, you stupid robot, who am I and who I'm meeting with? You're dead, you understand that? You have no clue about me!*

Such thoughts started coming from my subconscious and filling my consciousness.

*Stop immediately!* I heard a strict voice in my mind. *Stop, if you want me to teach you again!*

*Timeless?*

*Of course. What's the point of me giving you the knowledge if you then use it for evil purposes? Maybe Naia is right: your species is really too dangerous.*

*Please forgive me, I'm sorry...*

*It's not about that. You have to know who you are.*

*Who... am I?* I asked in my thoughts. I was still running and Naia wasn't paying too much attention to me.

*I can't explain that to you now. Come when you're done running. As usual. And if I ever hear you thinking such nonsense again... you can say goodbye to me right now.*

*No, no, it's all right. I'll come. Today. Thank you very much,* I thought humbly. The line was already dead.

## XXIII. THE TEST

I RAN UP TO THE GNOSIS' STATUE. I waited, as usual, for Timeless to guide me and tell me when the cameras would be pointed away from the entrance, so I could sneak in. I waited for the instructions, but the line wouldn't open.

*Timeless? How do I get in?* I tried to focus my thoughts on her. It didn't work. If she wanted to, she could completely hide her thoughts from me. And the line would evaporate into nothing. If I hadn't seen the small door at the base of the statue, I would have start to think I had dreamt about the whole thing.

*Of course I didn't just dreamt about it*, I thought. *How do I feel? What do I know? How am I thinking? Of course everything is true! It has to be!*

After I had circled the statue ten times, it finally occurred to me that Timeless might be testing me. Was I going to get in without her help? Considering the angry talk she had given me before, this kind of a test would make perfect sense. Cruel, but sensible. Well, that was OK too.

I stepped away from the statue and sat on the nearest bench. *How many cameras do I have to find? Ten?* Soon I had to deal with all the negative thoughts and ideas that resurfaced from my subconscious.

What if I failed? One single camera was enough for them to tie me to the bed again… One single wrong move. Fear filled my body. *Weak kidneys, huh?* I joked. *There's no time for that, Zyna. Find the solution. The feelings you're experiencing are a reflection of your body, nothing more.*

I calmed down and started looking for the cameras. The first three, installed on nearby houses, were pretty obvious. As I watched them, I noticed they were synchronized. They all rotated with the same speed in the same direction.

The next two were more interesting. They were installed at the top of the square, pointing vertically down. They followed all moving objects, therefore they weren't synchronized. Each was pointing in its own direction.

*How did Timeless know when to give me a sign?* I thought helplessly. I sat on the bench considering if I should just go home. Confusion. What is confusion? The weakness of the heart. Aimlessness. My machine had obviously broken down again. *This is just my body*, I thought again. *Just my body. If I want to use it, I mustn't follow it – it must follow me!*

I felt relieved and energized once more. I focused on my goal again, imagining Timeless waiting for me inside the statue, giggling.

*Serves me right*, I sighed, *for giving in to negative thoughts…* I'd never have thought the consequences could be fatal…

I spotted the sixth camera. It was on the top of the square's northernmost building. It could be said that it had an overview of everything.

*That's impossible!* I thought angrily. *Isn't there a single camera in this town I could avoid?!*

I became impatient and really angry, because I couldn't get to the bottom of this thing. I couldn't and I wouldn't! *Why should I risk my life again? I'm saved and I have some knowledge. Maybe that's a sign for me to go ahead by myself. Without her help. She doesn't want to help me anyway. She withdrew into herself and that's it.*

I could feel my heartbeat increase and a part of me stopped. Why was I so anxious? If the things I thought about represented what I really wanted, I wouldn't feel such anxiety. Anger. It was about my body again. My liver, to be exact. I could feel how precisely everything Timeless had taught me was intertwined with reality. It was one thing to talk about it.

And something completely different to act on one's own.

I focused my thoughts again. *I'll make it. There's no point in getting angry just because I'm not satisfied with my abilities. It'd be much better to improve my abilities instead of trying to place the blame outside myself…*

I counted the cameras again. The three that rotated… The two on the top… The sixth one on the northern side…

On the southern, eastern and western sides I noticed the seventh, eighth and ninth cameras. These too were placed very strategically and could catch anybody.

*All right. Let's say I catch the first three. If I move precisely when they're pointing away from me, it could work. How do I outsmart the top two? If something started happening on the edge of the square, they'd probably point in that direction. At least one of them. That means that something should happen on each side of the square, causing a lot of movement to distract the top cameras. If that happened I'd have to wait for the first three cameras to turn away and then slip into the statue. But there are also the cameras pointing in all directions of the compass… what do they record? What is their range? Are they accurate? Besides, I haven't spotted the tenth camera yet…* I was racking my brains, but I couldn't find the solution. I was thinking and thinking…

*Wait a minute,* I thought. *Thinking. A lot of thoughts. The spleen. Once again I can't realize something because I'm being obstructed by my own body…*

Once again I was subjected to my own body's limitations.

I decided to really follow the rules. *Why do I have the knowledge if I don't use it?*

I closed my eyes and relaxed. I was truly ready. I relaxed and imagined peace. Just that. Peace. Peace in my body. In my organs. I listened to the sounds around me…

*I'll make it. Where there's a strong insecurity, there's also a great strength. I believe. I truly believe. Universe, help me, please.*

I listened to the people walking by. I could hear the fluttering of

Skaturian cranes flying over the square's domes… The clatter of brace-lets as the children were playing with lasers in the southern part of the square. I also heard a low buzzing sound that was constantly present in the background… I could hear it was connected with all the other cameras…

I opened my eyes. A small, round metallic thing was rotating on the statue's head, on the mayor's helmet. As I looked closer, I recognized it… the tenth camera!

I remained calm and kept watching the cameras like they were my friends. Like they weren't a life-threatening menace. They were just cam-eras. Recording the movement in this tiny part of the universe. Without them my life would've been less challenging. I loved them. And today they were about to present me with the new ability… how to get inside the statue without being caught by one of them!

I was still sitting and my eyes rested on my newfound friends. The buzzing sound was moving away and then again closer. Moving away and moving closer… I felt a true connection with my surroundings. Absolutely nothing frightening was waiting for me. My future was bright. Just bright and nothing else. The test I was given wasn't so hard that I couldn't solve it. Otherwise I wouldn't have got it.

In the end the cameras were all I could see. Those round devices, each pointing in its own direction… Four groups of beings were crossing the square. I was surrounded by numerous beings, each rushing in its own direction… Suddenly, I felt the impulse inside me.

*Now.*

I knew. I calmly walked to the door, stepped through it and closed it behind me.

## XXIV. EGO

As I locked the door behind me, I heard a voice in my head again. *Excellent, you've come. That means you're ready.*

I turned around and saw Timeless standing behind me.

*Has it been as easy as it seemed?*

I smiled. *Of course not.*

*Can you feel now what it means to practice – to really implement the things I've been teaching you?*

I nodded.

*Now you also know who you are. You fall under the influence of positive as well as negative energy very quickly. You'll have to learn to open up to the positive frequencies that are helping you and protect yourself from the low frequencies that are destroying you. The fight you were fighting in front of the statue would've been a lot shorter if you had known who you were. If you had known how to stand up to your own body.*

I felt slight disappointment – since I was very proud of myself for successfully passing the test.

*Much too slowly,* Timeless was strict.

*And another thing: being proud of the past is a major obstacle. Imagine, how a musician would play a composition if he stopped after every note he played, feeling proud of it? You should always look ahead. There's no time for looking back.*

It hurt, even though I knew she was right.

*That's your ego,* she thought. *I've already told you that it tends to take hold of your body and that it hurts when you want to get rid of it. But to talk about it is one thing…*

*… and to feel it is something quite different,* I finished her thought.

*That's true. It's time now that we started doing something really fun.*

*What's that?* I was curious.

*A new dimension of comprehension that nobody on this planet knows about. Well, almost nobody.*

We sat down and she started teaching me…

## XXV. A NEW DIMENSION

W*E COULD WORK ON ENHANCING YOUR ABILITIES BUT, UNFORTUNATELY, we don't have time for that*, she thought.
*First, try to relax.*

I closed my eyes. Soon I got an interesting feeling that Timeless started walking around the room. A shadow flashed past me. I was surprised that she decided to leave in the middle of the lesson. I slightly opened one eye and peeped in her direction.

Incredibly, she was sitting completely still – and still facing me! I closed my eyes and again somebody went past my body, this time in the other direction. Like somebody was walking around me. Once again I slightly opened my eyes, but couldn't see anybody except my sitting mentor.

*Haven't I told you to relax?* I heard the voice inside my head. I froze immediately. I didn't realize that she could see me.

*Of course I can see you. Soon you'll understand how. Provided that you follow my instructions, that is.*

I closed my eyes and relaxed. I had no other option anyway. Nothing happened for the first five minutes. It was just me, thinking about what might happen. When I finally managed to quiet down my thoughts, I felt like I started separating from my own body. Like the body I'd been living in, wasn't quite mine anymore. This weird feeling intensified and soon I felt pressure in my head. I started to levitate.

*Relax*, I heard her firm and clear instructions.

She had lifted me at least two feet above the ground.

*Stretch your legs and stand up.*

I did as I was told. When I opened my eyes, I saw an entirely different world. I saw the energy of my body that was still peacefully sitting on the ground, the heat of the room, I saw through metal.

*What do you see?* she asked me.

*I don't know how to explain this*, I thought in amazement. *I see EVERYTHING. Like I wasn't using my eyes before.*

*Just pay attention to this*, she said and pointed towards the glittering cord that connected my material and my non-material left leg. She quickly untied the cord from my sitting body and skillfully wrapped it around my non-material left leg. The whole thing somewhat resembled a fashionable glittering shoestring.

*Now you can really travel – anywhere you want*, she said.

*Really? Even to Kairon?*

She knew this question would arise.

*Yes, even to him*, she said reconciling.

I looked at her pleadingly.

*Please?*

Timeless didn't answer me. She stepped on the wall, effortlessly defying the law of gravity.

*Now you do it!*

I followed her example and fell down twice.

*Do you think your soul has anything to do with the gravity in this room…?* she asked smiling.

*No…*

*Then free yourself of gravity!* she said and stepped on the ceiling. *Imagine that it's possible and it will be possible. Everything's possible*, she said with conviction.

*Everything's possible, everything's possible, everything's possible*, I was repeating to myself as I stepped on the wall.

I slipped again.

*What if I told you that after the lesson we might visit… Kairon?* she asked me smiling.

I was focused in an instant. There had to be a way for me to overcome the obstacle that was evidently just a product of my mind. I started imagining that I'd succeeded. I stepped on the wall. I made three steps. I was clinging like crazy to the thought that I was still there. That I was standing on the wall. Soon I moved towards the ceiling. I put my right foot on the ceiling and then joined the left one. I considered opening my eyes, but was afraid of losing my concentration.

*Open them,* she thought, *and know where you're standing. Be firmly convinced that you'll make it.*

I put my feet onto the ceiling again and opened my eyes. Timeless was standing right in front of me, also on the ceiling, and I had a feeling that the two of us were standing normally, while the rest of the room was turned upside down.

*And now come down,* she thought and gently somersaulted to the ground.

I followed her. Even though I landed a bit harder, I still managed to stay on my feet.

*Are you aware of what just happened?* she asked.

I looked at her.

*What?*

*Why you couldn't do it at first, and then, when I mentioned Kairon, you did it without a problem? You need to understand why.*

*Because of my interest…?*

*Exactly. When you were practicing standing on the wall, the goal as such didn't mean anything to you. It'd have been 'cool' to master such a skill, but that was all.*

I thought it was fun hearing her use such an expression.

*But when you heard the name Kairon, which interests you more than anything else in the world, your interest was suddenly transferred to the task you had to do. Standing on the wall suddenly became your life's purpose. Your interest in performing the task increased tenfold, hundredfold.*

In the beginning her explanation seemed simple, but now I wasn't sure anymore I was following her.

*You have to have an interest in everything you want to achieve in life. Otherwise you won't make it. A strong interest. Understand?*

I understood. I felt the difference in the power of my actions in the beginning and in the end. And everything came down to Kairon.

*Wrong. YOU are the one responsible for everything. How much Kairon means to you is your business.*

She was right again.

*One more little detail and we can be on our way.*

*And that is?*

Timeless appeared in front of me in an instant and in the next second she was standing next to the wall on the other side of the room.

*Soul teleportation,* she declared. *It works exactly the same as walking on the wall, only you have to imagine you're in some other place. And to save us some time we'd otherwise spend on your failed attempts: when you learn how to do this, we'll go to the city of Hax! To Hax 231, to be precise.*

I was beside her in an instant.

*Excellent,* she thought. *Do you remember what that round house looked like…?*

## XXVI. THE VISIT

W E TOOK EACH OTHER'S HANDS AND CLOSED OUR EYES. I could clearly see the round dome with the glass frontage in my memory. The interior was metallic and round. On the sliding front door it said: Hax 231.

We were there in an instant. It was nighttime on the other side of the planet and there were moons and stars shining in the sky. We stepped on the round wall and took a short walk.

*Here*, said Timeless and set her foot inside. I followed her. Or should I say I followed my extra strong interest.

It was dark in the room, but I could see Kairon's bed. As we approached it, I noticed that only his body was in it; there was no sign of life, no sign of his soul.

*Behind you*, I heard his soft voice. I turned around.

*Kairon!*

We hugged and although the feeling was entirely different than before, when we were in our bodies, I felt happiness and love throughout my entire being. I kissed him and felt like I was sending him pure light through my lips. He hugged me even tighter and it seemed like we found ourselves in some sort of a fusion… It felt like I was Kairon, like I was both of us. Like we were one.

*Well, lovebirds*, I heard Timeless' voice that woke us from our intoxicating fusing, *this was supposed to be a business meeting…*

*You'll have a very difficult time achieving that*, replied Kairon smiling.

*You two know each other…?*

*What did you think? That I was standing around doing nothing?* he gently asked me. *I've been longing for you too. And Timeless responded to that… strong interest.*

*More of a desperate cry for help, but let's not dwell on the details,* our mentor corrected him.

I looked at her and I could feel that she sensed a question in my eyes. *I wanted to surprise you,* she explained.

*You've succeeded,* I smiled. *But I've earned another minute with my chosen one…*

I hugged him again and this time he held me even tighter. He lifted me off the ground and we stopped in mid-air. When he kissed me, another stream of light passed through me. We reveled in each other's presence – more than ever before. Deeper. And maybe… a bit more mature. In silence that surrounded us, I forgot all the sadness and everything I had to go through to be with him again. I simply enjoyed the silence and the light we shared. We started whirling in the air and only after a few circles and loop-the-loops we became aware of the fact that we weren't alone.

*Well, all right,* I concluded when he put me on the ground.

*Let's start with the meeting!*

# XXVII. THE TASK

*A*s *you've already found out, you're the only Earthlings on this planet that haven't been inoculated with the Kanter serum.*
I obligingly raised my hand.

*What is this serum and where does it come from? It namely reminds me of…*

*Yes, of the name of the planet. That's true. It's called that because that's where it's used the most,* Timeless answered me.

She continued with the explanation. *Planet Kanter is, generally speaking, supposed to be a planet for depositing. But I prefer to call it the »Planet of Oblivion«. There are vast depository areas on this planet, where beings whose planets have been disintegrated, are deposited. Their minds are emptied in special depository coffins, so they wouldn't repeat the same mistakes that caused the disintegration of their planets. To put it in the nutshell, their memories are deleted. At the same time their bodies are supplied with all the essential nutrients.*

We were surprised.

*Isn't there any other way…?* asked Kairon.

*We've tried every possible way,* explained Timeless, *but without success. The human species has been especially obstinate.*

*You've tried… does that mean that Kanter is your idea?*

*Kanter is a common project planet of both the Rulers and the Darkened. The Rulers take care that there's always more light and peace than darkness in the universe. They are responsible for maintaining the balance in the universe. The Darkened carry out orders and are executors of extreme acts. Their vibration is much lower than the vibration of the Rulers, yet there are common issues on which both forces must come to an agreement. Kanter is one of such issues. The beings are allowed to live, but they must forget absolutely everything that reminds them of their own planets. If they knew what they'd left behind, there'd be too much grief and chaos on the planets the rockets had brought them to. That's why all the inhabitants of this planet are under the influence of the Kanter serum. So they wouldn't run amok like you had, Zyna.*

Not wanting to be biased, she also turned to the other side.

*Or you, Kairon.*

*Then why… why we don't have the serum?* I asked.

*There is a very interesting explanation for that. Because you claimed – like everybody else that had been sent here from the planet of oblivion – that you didn't remember anything. The Ska-robots recognized the correct answer and concluded that you'd been 'cleansed'. But in fact you'd come directly from your home planet – planet Earth.*

We stood there in silence. I experienced another memory flashback. *Me and Kairon – in our respective rockets. We're looking at each other through the glass and find the entire thing pretty amusing. Outside our rockets there's a black-haired boy waving at us and making funny faces, like it's some sort of a game…*

*He's the one you have to find,* she instructed us.

*His name is Derek Blake. It's because of him that you're the only ones on this planet that might change the future for the better. But first you have to save him. That's why I've been training you.*

We looked at each other and smiled.

*It's pure luck,* thought Kairon, *that we're so important for the future. Because otherwise I don't know how I'd get to you…*

*All right, lovebirds,* said Timeless. *Now you know what your task is. Any questions?*

Before I could tear my eyes off of Kairon's she already continued: *then we can conclude for today!*

*Wait!* I said quickly. *We will come back, won't we…?*

She rolled her eyes. *Of course. You'll get tired of each other.*

He caressed my hair and hugged me. *I'll never get tired of you*, he thought. Soon Timeless and me found ourselves in the room beneath the metallic statue, next to our bodies. As we reattached ourselves to them, I felt intense peace and happiness. At the same time I believed for the first time in my life that I had more powerful weapon than any other inhabitant of Skatur: genuine knowledge and pure love.

## XXVIII. THE INVITATION

THE NEXT DAY TIMELESS ASKED ME TO SOON BRING NAIA WITH ME.
»But Naia is a robot,« I resisted, fearing the disclosure of my secret learning.
»Exactly.«

»She's been programmed to pass on every – but every single bit of information. Including where we've been studying.«

»Do you really think I'd want to expose you to such danger?«

I thought about how I had to find an appropriate moment to enter the room beneath the statue by myself. That too was dangerous. Partly joking and partly seriously I replied:

»Maybe.«

»You don't have to be afraid. You'll namely soon realize that Naia could be much more helpful to us than it seems at first sight.«

»How...?«

»Every being that moves around planet Skatur has its body, even robots. Do you agree?«

»Yes, I do, but...«

»The difference is that some bodies are of technical and the others of biological nature. The first type needs an outside energy source for its operation – like the solar energy or electricity, while the other type needs the energy from food and drink, as well as the soul, of course, which can be charged with the energy of the universe. Can you follow?«

»Barely.«

Timeless took a deep breath, which she didn't really need. She must have thought I was being a bit slow on the uptake.

»It's important that you understand this. If you take energy away from a robot, you're left with an empty casing. If you take away somebody else's soul, you're left with a corps. You can last a month without food. A few days without water. And not a second without energy!«

»What are you trying to say?«

»I want to give you a hint, how important the energy that fuels us really is.«

I pondered over that for a while.

»Bring Naia with you tomorrow and you'll understand more easily. I'll help you get in safely.«

Although I didn't understand everything she told me that day, I decided to still trust her.

»All right. Sure. I'll bring her.«

»Excellent,« she concluded and I could feel that she was preparing a special surprise for me…

## XXIX. UNCERTAINTY

»NAIA…« I BEGAN TIMIDLY THE NEXT DAY WHEN WE FINISHED RUNNING. »Would you like to… go to the city center with me today?«
»What for?« she asked.

»Ah, just like that. I'd like to show you something.« I couldn't think of anything better to say.

At home I changed, while the robot was waiting for me by the front door. She told my parents we were going to the city center together and they were very pleased. They never liked it me going to the city by myself. They were glad that I finally invited Naia to come along.

»Zyna, are you done?« she called out.

»Yes.« I came running to the front door and we went off together. I though about how I was going to get her inside the statue the whole time. And more importantly, how I was going to persuade her not to say anything to anybody about it.

»Naia?« I glanced at her as we were walking. »Have… have you been programmed to tell everything to everybody all the time? I mean, let's say that… I'd like to tell you a secret.«

»Do you have a secret?« she answered my question with the question.

»Well, let's say that I did,« I broached my subject again. »And let's say that I confided in you. Would you tell my parents?«

»Absolutely,« she said with conviction. »We robots keep no secrets. Especially not from other beings.«

I was pretty desperate. »But… then why didn't you want to reveal certain information to me until I was eighteen?« I was clutching at straws now. »You've kept secrets from me!«

»That was different,« she rebutted. »I've been programmed so that I couldn't tell you certain things.«

I sighed.

»Well, if you do have a secret, you better tell me quickly so we can clear it up. It's not nice to keep secrets, you know?«

*And now this too,* I thought helplessly.

*You're trying too hard,* I heard Timeless' voice in my head. Her presence gave me such a sense of relief. Naia and I were quickly approaching the square now.

*What do I do? She'll tell my parents everything, and who knows who else,* I summed up.

*Just relax. Tell her. Tell her everything. And let me take care of everything else.*

*Well, all right.*

»Well, anything?« she looked at me in anticipation.

»Well,« I swallowed hard and prepared for the most senseless thing I'd ever done. »I've been seeing somebody.«

»A human?« she asked harshly.

I thought about Timeless' special abilities. She probably wasn't a regular human. »Not really, at least I think she is not human,« I said. »And these meetings haven't been romantic in nature!« I quickly added.

»What then? Soon you'll have to choose your mate,« she reminded me.

Just thinking about choosing a being from this planet – a schilar, a violet orruwin, a hermaphrodite, or a lizard – made my skin crawl.

»I've still got enough time for those things. Today I wanted to show you something completely different.«

»What?« she asked with interest. Again I became reluctant to tell her anything.

*Continue,* said Timeless in my head. *We don't have all day…*

*I'm trying,* I resisted.

We came to the statue.

»I wanted to show you...« I could feel the sweat running down my back, »this statue. Ta-ta!«

»I'm familiar with this statue. The statue of our Leader Gnosis. Are you all right, Zyna? Why are you showing me a statue that everybody knows?«

*Come on, Zyna. The cameras will soon be in the right positions...* I heard Timeless.

»Well, everybody knows the statue. But nobody knows that one can enter this statue... through a small door.«

»How do you know that?« she asked. »Nobody knows that. You shouldn't know that either.«

»You know?« I asked completely surprised.

»I have a map of allowed and forbidden places on my hard drive. And this one is forbidden for you.« She took me by my arm. »Come on, we have to talk to the authorities.«

*Timeless, help me,* I cried out in my thoughts.

*You're holding hands,* she answered calmly. *On my signal drag her over here.*

»Don't be stubborn, Zyna. Come on,« she seized my arm harder.

Timeless started counting down. *Three, two, one...*

»Naia, we'll go there immediately. But first come with me!«

*Now!*

I quickly dragged her with me through the door and immediately bolted them.

# XXX. THE BODY OF THE ROBOT

»FORBIDDEN PLACE. Forbidden place. Forbidden place.« Naia was stuck in some sort of frenzy mode. It was obvious that without a good signal even the robots didn't function properly in these places.

*Now we have to silence you,* thought Timeless and placed a hand on her. The Ska-robot became silent immediately.

I was perplexed. *How did you do that?*

*You haven't asked the right question. The question is what did I do it with,* explained Timeless.

*All right. What did you did it with?*

*You'll see soon enough.* She sat on the ground with her legs crossed. *Join me,* she motioned.

We relaxed and left our bodies. We could put our minds at ease again. In this state nobody could see or hear us.

*And now we can take a closer look at what robots are made of,* she began.

Again I was surprised by how many things I could now notice about Naia that I wasn't able to before. I could see the heat concentrating around certain parts of metal. I could see thinner and thicker wires intertwining inside the shell. I found it interesting that they were concentrated in the head and heart areas.

*All robots are experimental copies of living beings. However, Naia only has a physical body. Without any other content. She's powered by an external energy source, that's why her body – when in a place without a signal – resembles a corpse. It's lifeless. It just is. You, on the other hand – as you've already noticed – have several bodies: the physical, the ethereal, the spiritual. You don't need an external signal to function. That's your advantage. That's why you'll always have the advantage!* she concluded with conviction.

I just couldn't believe how subdued Naia became. Even though she stopped functioning, little lights in her body kept flickering.

*Her body is in the standby mode. As soon as you'll bring her out, she'll remember everything you talked about.*
I flinched again.

*Except,* she emphasized, *if you do what we are about to do,* and calmed me down.

*Some observation will be needed,* she warned me. *Study her well – have a look where the thickest wires are – that's her nervous system.*

The main, thickest wire ran down the middle of the body; it started to thicken by a curvature similar to a tailbone and ended in the head. Like some sort of a spine. Attached to it were the two main nerve clusters – cerebral and cardiac, although these names were appropriate only in view of their positions. Naia didn't have any human-like organs. The medium-sized wires extended into both arms and legs.

*The main nerve clusters are the heart and the head,* she summed up my thoughts. *The heart part is assigned to imitate human comprehension, even human feelings to some extent. It also adjusts the emotional maturity to the age and distributes energy throughout the nervous system. The head part takes care of the motion coordination and contains a hard drive and an evaluation system.*

*An evaluation system...?*

*Every robot contains a program that classifies the data according to its settings. And each program can be modified or adapted. If you're familiar with its codes, of course. Here, once again, comes in the rule that extends beyond the boundaries of the knowledge of robotics...*

*And that is?*

*If you have the RIGHT knowledge, you have all the codes!*

I had absolutely no idea what she had meant by that.

*That's impossible! Nobody can have all the codes!* I contradicted.

*Considering how long I've been teaching you, you should know by now that absolutely everything's possible,* she replied disappointed. *Come on, I'd like to invite you to a demonstration!*

## XXXI. DEMONSTRATION

Timeless approached Naia. She entered the robot's body with her soul and kept still for a while. I noticed that the light flickered differently than usually from time to time. It seemed that Timeless' soul and Naia's body were getting to know each other.

After a few minutes of standstill she untied a shining thread from her left leg that connected her material body with the ethereal one. She fastened it in the middle of Naia's cardiac nerve cluster. From there on the light spread across all the wires – thin and thick – and ultimately hit the head. Naia's body opened its eyes.

Once again I was speechless. Then Timeless started moving Naia's arms, legs, the head...

*Do you see now?* she thought while Naia's face smiled calmly. *This way you can access all the programs. You get to choose what to tell the others and what not. The robot's evaluation system is in your hands. You can classify the information and save it as you see fit. When Naia wakes up, she'll resume where you left off.*

*Unbelievable,* I thought when I saw Naia moving under Timeless' guidance. Naia with Timeless' soul.

*Can you please erase that part when we got to the square and Naia decided to take me to the authorities? That'd be really nice...* I thought.

*Actually, no,* she answered with a smile. *You'll take care of that part.*

*Me?*

*It's not that complicated,* she reassured me while softly walking around the room. It was still interesting to watch her: a robot with human soul. I couldn't take my eyes off her.

*But I have to warn you, the body structure is completely different,* she added.

*What do you mean by that?*

*The body you'll connect to is emptier than yours that you're used to.*

*Emptier?*

*It has no internal organs, its weight is completely different, as is the nervous layout of the system. This body has no energy centers or meridians like yours. At first the feeling will be slightly weird, you have to know that. And be careful not to give in to reflexes.*

*Reflexes?*

*When you enter a robot's body for the first time,* she continued while still walking around me in Naia's body, *you enter the body whose composition is far less dense than yours, and made of different material. Since you're not used to it, stimuli cause reflex reactions. The hands are heavier, as are the legs. The head and the cardiac cluster work entirely differently. Be prepared for that,* she warned me.

Now I could hardly wait to try it for myself.

*May I try?* I was impatient.

*Take your time,* she thought. Meanwhile she used her thoughts to direct the shining thread out of the robot's cardiac cluster, then took it and fastened it again to her left leg.

She stood still for a while in the robot's body, like she was respectfully saying goodbye to it.

*Why did you do that?* I asked her when she was finished.

*Because the senses of respect and acclimatization are very important. For the electricity flow inside the robot, as well as for the substance of your soul. If you connected or disconnected too quickly, it might be dangerous, especially for you.*

*May I begin now?* I was impatient.

*At first just stand inside the body for a while. Then follow only my instructions,* she emphasized. The tone of her voice indicated that I was about to do something that might be dangerous…

## XXXII. THE CONSCIOUSNESS OF THE ROBOT

I ENTERED NAIA'S BODY. Earlier I noticed the flashing of the electric current through the wires. This time it prickled me from time to time. It felt like some sort of tingling all over my body. But different. Electric tingling.

This feeling was becoming stronger and stronger.

*Surrender to it,* thought Timeless. *Except it as your own.*

I could increasingly feel the electric buzzing on my skin, which was now metallic. Made of some sort of soft steel alloy, covered with a special, abrasion-preventing coating. The coating was made of a substance mixture so strong that a house could be dropped on me and I wouldn't break.

*And now slowly connect to it,* she instructed me. *It's important that you imagine entering into the very heart of the wire cluster. Into the center. Your shining thread will follow your thought.*

I took the cord and put it near the nerve cluster. I imagined it already being inside. The shining thread gently slipped past the first wires in the cluster and stopped in its center.

*Now imagine the installation,* she thought clearly. *Sheer installation!*

It was helpful that I saw a socket and a plug in my mind. Something that can be connected. Suddenly, my soul and my metallic body shook violently. I could feel the head that was much more complicated than mine – and much lighter at the same time. Since it was lighter than my human head, I raised it too much and it leaned backwards too much. The entire body fell to the ground.

As I wanted to get up, I raised my light arms much too high. The reflex then transferred to my legs, where I experienced some sort of convulsion. While my body was on the ground, my feet were helplessly kicking in the air, trying to walk.

*Lie down*, Timeless ordered me, *and calm your body down!*

I lay down. I had no other option anyway. It seemed simple, but it wasn't really. As I was lying on the ground, the tingling sensation returned and it seemed somewhat regular. Like it was a substitute for heartbeat.

I closed my metallic eyes, which saw the room much clearer than the eyes in my biological body, and tried to focus. I wanted to inhale air, which I didn't need. As I was gasping for air, all I felt was the opening and closing of my metallic jaws. I wanted to swallow the saliva, but there wasn't any. Every single function I was used to when I was attached to my own body, simply vanished. Only the slight and regular buzzing of the heart remained.

*Now focus and remember what happened when you came to the square*, she gave me the next instruction.

As I was trying to remember us coming to the square, I didn't think about myself and Naia anymore. I thought about myself, Naia, and the girl I had been walking with, Zyna. It was interesting seeing myself through the eyes of a robot. Like I wasn't myself anymore, in a way.

*Excellent*, Timeless praised me. *Now remember the whole scene!*

WE ARRIVE AT THE SQUARE.

»Well, anything?« I say. People are complicated when it comes to feelings.

»Well,« she answers, »I've been seeing somebody.«

That isn't right. She shouldn't meet in secret. Especially not with

friends of her own species. Gathering information. »A human?«
I get the answer. »Not really, at least I think not,« she says and the answer
seems strange. »And these meetings haven't been romantic in nature!«

»What then? Soon you'll have to choose your mate,« I encourage her.
It's nice that she's realized that her place isn't with the male of her species.
The subject isn't a threat anymore. Mission accomplished.

»I've still got enough time for those things. Today I wanted to show
you something completely different,« she continues.

»What?« I ask. I'll enter the information in the 'Report' folder.

We come to the statue. Her hesitation attracts my attention even more.
Dilated pupils – fear. Increased heartbeat. Her neuro-image is above expected. Increased body heat. Sensing increased perspiration on her skin.

»I wanted to show you…« she's still hesitating. The subject is obviously
still dangerous. Suspicious behavior ends with pointing at the object.
»This statue. Ta-ta!«

I turn on the worried tone of voice. I'm hoping she'll follow my voice. A
mistake probably occurred during the inoculation with the Kanter serum.
Repeat inoculation needed. »I'm familiar with this statue. The statue of
our Leader Gnosis. Are you all right, Zyna? Why are you showing me
the statue that everybody knows?«

»Well, everybody knows the statue. But nobody knows that one can
enter this statue… through a small door,« she continues. I'm scanning.
The image corresponds with the forbidden place. The subject is highly
dangerous. It has access to the meeting place of the planet's Leaders.

»How do you know that?« I ask. »Nobody knows that. You shouldn't
know that either.«

»You know?« she asks. Subject Zyna is highly dangerous. I answer her
question, then take her to the authorities.

»I have a map of allowed and forbidden places on my hard drive. And this one is forbidden for you.« I take her by her arm. »Come on, we have to talk to the authorities.« Subject Zyna resists. I will turn on the alarm in thirty seconds. Take her to the authorities.

»Don't be stubborn, Zyna. Come on,« I seize her harder. Take her to the authorities.

Subject Zyna pulls me towards herself, which she usually does not do.

»Naia, we'll go there immediately.« Subject agrees, that is good. »But first come with me!«

Dragged through the door. Forbidden place. Forbidden place.


I opened my eyes again. I noticed Timeless again, but I saw less than before. My eyes perceived the material and less and less what Timeless referred to as *the soul*.

*Your eyes tend to perceive just the material world – like the eyes of other robots*, explained Timeless. *But I have to praise your excellent memory.*

*Thank you, but I really don't want to remember this*, I reminded her.

*It's time for a change then*, she thought smilingly.

## XXXIII. THE TWIST

N*OW SIT UP AND CLOSE YOUR EYES.*
I crossed my metallic legs, which made an interesting sound when they slightly rubbed against each other, and sat up. I closed my eyes.

*The memory that you have now has completely different characteristics than human memory. You can actually MARK this memory.*

When I heard that word, the image in my head immediately turned violet. Like I'd marked the section of the movie I'd just lived through. I was ready to do anything with it. I could process, delete or edit it.

*We'll simply delete it and record a new one,* Timeless thought firmly.

*Delete.* Slight buzzing in my head cluster and it was gone. We arrived at the square and from then on I remembered nothing more. Timeless calmly continued.

*Listen to my voice and imagine what I'm saying.* The sound of her thoughts was penetrating and convincing. It was being imprinted in my consciousness like a powerful memory. I was led by her voice and I imagined what she said creating a new memory.

W*E ARRIVE AT THE SQUARE.* Zyna is behaving properly and she is relaxed. »I love being in this square,« she says. I agree. It's beautiful. »Yes. It's beautiful,« I concur.

»Can we please go to the clothes store?« she asks.

»Of course,« I say. It's nice that she's interested in fashion. Having tried on a couple of items, she doesn't buy anything. She's right. We haven't seen any nice clothes today.

»How are you feeling?« I check. Subject Zyna is lively and calms down.

»Good,« she says. The Kanter serum works excellently. Her thermal image is normal, her pupils are medium-sized, and her neuro-psychological condition is stable.

»Do you still yearn sometimes?« I check.

»Yearn for what?« she asks.

Complete amnesia regarding her human friend. The serum has exceeded all expectations. One-hundred-percent deletion of last month's data and emotional release. Subject Zyna is no longer dangerous. Report to the management.

»Nothing,« I answer. »Life is too beautiful to be polluted with yearning.«

»I agree,« she says. We reach the Gnosis Dral statue. We sit on the bench next to it.

»Thank you for being at my side,« she says. Then she leans on my shoulder and closes her eyes. I imitate human emotions. I close my eyes.

*Excellent*, thought Timeless. *It's time for you to disconnect. Don't forget to save that memory*, she warned me.

I saved it.

*Now don't move your body. Keep your eyes closed. You mustn't sense anything else. Otherwise we'll create a new memory.*

I understood.

When I disconnected my shining thread from the cardiac cluster, I felt relieved. The danger of creating another memory was over. I spent the next few minutes just being in the metallic body, saying goodbye to the electric signals that represented the beating of my substitute heart just a few minutes ago.

Timeless instructed me to slowly move away from the body. I stepped away and felt free again. I wasn't trapped in the electronic circuit anymore.

Then she took some time to explain the development of robots and Ska-robots to me.

*Even the people on planet Earth had and used robots, because robots made their lives significantly easier,* thought Timeless.

*But soon the extraordinarily fast development of robotics went so far that the society split into two parts. One part was represented by the people who consciously trained to attain a higher frequency state and with it – as you have already noticed – they surpassed the abilities of any robot. These people were also highly creative. They had discovered a way to prevent the aging of their bodies with the help of additional energy from the universe. With the larger quantity of energy they had acquired, they helped everybody who was prepared to listen to them. Their abilities were very highly developed and similar to the abilities of the first Lemurians that lived on the planet Earth. Flying and teleportation, which they had developed, were used exclusively for good purposes.*

*The other part of society was represented by the people who had lower abilities than the machines. Their jobs had been taken over by the humanoid Assims. This group of people was heavily subjected to negative vibrations. They wouldn't admit to themselves that their abilities were too low and that they just lacked knowledge. So they started blaming the first group of people. They became extremely primitive and very easily manageable. Regardless of how hard the first group of people was trying to bring awareness to the planet, the divide continued to grow. Longing for happiness was growing stronger. Out of the eternal desire to control as well as understand the power that human beings carry within them the Darkened resorted to the creation of a special memory card. And because the card provided happiness humans were longing for, and even enabled freer communication and clearer census, installing it into the nervous system became very popular… What owners of the new card didn't realize was a dark secret: the card actually owned them and not the other way around. Humans carrying built-in memory card became easily manageable. Naturally, the Darkened acquired services of those within political circles who could pass the legislation regarding the card. The use of the card was compulsory – exempt from it were only the co-called Happy Cities where people were equally lacking freedom – being confined to different classes based on their awareness level. And since every technology has its headquarters, so did the memory cards. One press of the button sufficed for the long-suppressed anger of card owners to surface and they created total chaos. They destroyed everything in their path. And when mankind started using atom bombs the decision was made to annihilate the planet.*

*We, the Rulers, were given the task to notify all the people with high level of consciousness that they needed to leave the planet if they wanted to survive. The majority of them did that. And some of them… stayed on the planet right until its obliteration. They were determined to help the planet somehow.*

*Were my parents among them…?* I asked carefully. I was prepared for any answer.

*Yes, Zyna. Your parents and Kairon's parents too.*

I looked away. They wanted to save the planet. They wanted to help. *Did they want that more than knowing me…?*

*Don't think like that, Zyna. Sadness is a very destructive emotion. Especially because there's still a way to rectify certain things.*

*But how?* I asked bewildered. *Our parents are dead!*

*If you carry out the task you've been given, you may change something,* she tried to encourage me. *Come now, it's time we took the robot out. The hour's up.*

## XXXIV. A DANGEROUS ROMANCE

WHEN TIMELESS ASCERTAINED THAT ALL THE CAMERAS WERE FACING suitable directions, she helped me carry the robot to the bench. We said goodbye very quickly, because Naia started waking up.

She looked around and said: »Well, sleepyhead? Did you have enough of shopping?«

I remembered the memory recording Timeless and me saved in her memory and almost started laughing. Of course. That was the only thing Naia could remember.

»Yes, enough,« I faked exhaustion, »it's time we went home.«

When we got home, I did the final test: I went to my room, while Naia had a little chat with my parents. I left my room door ajar, so I could hear their conversation.

»Well, girls? Did you have a nice time?« asked mom.

»Very nice, thank you,« Naia answered. »We were trying on clothes, went to the main square... Zyna behaved very well.«

It was strange to hear such a statement – like I was a five-year-old. But now I knew and felt how Naia thought. I remembered the thought patterns passing through the wire clusters like equations... At first I was dangerous subject Zyna. Later I was well-behaved Zyna. When Naia left, I closed my room door and lay on the bed... So much had happened! I'd never have thought that life could be so full and so dangerous at the same time. That there'd be so many different options. And so many simple solutions. Suddenly I felt like I wasn't alone in the room anymore. I relaxed and detached from my body.

*I knew I couldn't surprise you!*

*Kairon!* I cried out and materialized next to him. He was on the other side of my room. *What are you doing here?*

*I've been watching you. And waiting for a lesson with Timeless.*

*Are we meeting here today?*

*Probably. I haven't told her I was going to see you, but she'll probably figure it out soon. I wanted to be alone with you for a while...*

I was touched by his sincerity. I too had been longing for a bit of privacy for some time. Even though I'd been missing his scent, his sheer presence was intoxicating enough. I snuggled up to him and brought my face close to his. As we kissed, the powerful wave of desire shook my entire being. I wanted to become one with him. Like hermaphrodites that inhabited our planet in large numbers. I slowly began to understand why they didn't need anybody, why they were much calmer and why they had much bigger abilities than the rest of the beings. Because they were fulfilled. When we were merging one into the other, it so happened that Kairon somehow entered into me. His soul merged with mine and I could feel that I finally became what I was meant to be. We existed in silence, indulging in the feeling of absolute peace. My substance started taking over his properties. And vice versa... Our merging was interrupted by a strict voice.

*Stop immediately!*

We heard Timeless' indignant voice and it felt like we'd been caught doing something forbidden.

*Do you realize how dangerous what you were just doing is?*

We looked at each other. *No,* I answered timidly.

*If you'd continued, you'd have to die,* she continued.

*Why?* asked Kairon.

*Just imagine. Two souls merging into one. Everything's good and well – very romantic. But to which body would such a soul return to? One body would have to die on the spot. And the other body wouldn't match the substance that would want to connect to it anymore. So the other body would die too, both would stay trapped in this dimension and who knows when they'd be allowed to reincarnate.* We understood.

*Only the highly advanced beings are allowed to perform such procedures and then only under the supervision of the Rulers. Do you understand?*

We nodded.

*Let's proceed with this meeting's agenda,* she continued.

*Kairon, the two of us will soon leave for the Left continent. And I have instructions for you, Zyna. Tomorrow we'll meet on the meadow bordering Hrylon Park. Bring Naia.*

*But that park has cameras too,* I remembered. *Are you sure that's a good idea?*

*Of course I am,* she reassured me. *As long as Naia's with you, we've got nothing to be afraid of. And the cameras won't even detect me. Be there and be prepared for a difficult practice. Have a good rest until tomorrow.*

*Agreed,* I thought. *See you tomorrow.*

*Have a nice day, darling,* said Kairon. We kissed once more and then he disappeared together with Timeless.

## XXXV. THE CONNECTION

The NEXT DAY I VERY QUICKLY CONVINCED NAIA THAT WE URGENTLY needed to take a walk to the Hrylon Park. She gladly came along. I was calm, because we told my parents where we were going and they were satisfied to see me spending time with my Ska-robot. After all, I had been strictly rejecting anything that wasn't from the planet Earth, including the robots, until recently.

They slowly started removing cameras from my room. Naia had reported to the authorities that I was a very well-behaved subject and that the inoculated serum was working excellently. She was almost proud – as much as such a mechanism could be – of her good influence on me. Not knowing, of course, that in reality it was me who influenced her memories and consciousness.

We arrived at the park and I asked Naia if we could relax for a minute. I spread out a little blanket that I'd brought with me and we sat on it. We relaxed. Naia closed her eyes too. I disconnected from my body and immediately noticed Timeless.

*Today's lesson will be a bit harder than usual,* she greeted me.

*Why?*

*Look at Naia. She's still connected. Since she's receiving a good signal, she's not as accessible as she was yesterday. We'll have to demagnetize her.*

Again, I was surprised. New challenges kept coming and coming.

*That's life. If you want new abilities, you have to face new challenges. But if you want, I can leave and…*

*No, no, it's all right! Stay, please,* I said, because I really wanted to know what was going to happen. I was also angry with myself, because I forgot how quickly Timeless was able to detect my thought vibration.

She smiled. She obviously caught my last thought as well.

She came closer and we approached Naia together. I could see that her nervous system was much more active than it was the day before. The wires that were almost empty a day ago and would blink only sporadically were now full of electricity.

*What now?* I thought. *How do I connect to her...?*

*It's simple,* thought Timeless. *You have to know where she's charged.*

She pointed towards the sensor on the nape of Naia's neck.

*This is where a robot receives energy. If you manage to demagnetize this center, you'll be able to freely connect to her, like you did yesterday. Or maybe even more easily. Try it. Bring your hand close to her.*

I brought my hand close to the nape of Naia's neck and felt a strong vibration of the electric current. It was spinning from left to right and was then sucked into the wires.

*If you wish to demagnetize this energy, you have to turn it in the opposite direction. That way the mechanism is disabled long enough for you to enter it. Then, when it charges and moves because of your soul's vibration, it doesn't matter anymore whether the external signal is present or not. Like with your body.*

I was surprised by this theory how easy it was to overpower the robots. They had always seemed so dangerous, omniscient and omnipotent. And now I had Naia's body in the palm of my hand and I could do with it whatever I wanted.

I was still holding my right hand next to the nape of Naia's neck and started thinking about the current that flows in the opposite direction.

*Don't think about it; become the current!* Timeless ordered me.

I concentrated even more. I began to imagine myself as a mixture of atoms moving inside Naia's wires. Only I changed the direction of my movement. I started to spin in the opposite direction.

*Excellent,* she encouraged me. *Continue!*

I started to reverse the flow of electricity even faster. I felt some sort of resistance that indicated that Naia was fighting. She didn't want to lose consciousness. She didn't know why she was shutting down or why the signal was changing. I was spinning in the opposite direction even harder. After a few minutes of fighting I was fairly tired.

*Don't ease up! Go beyond your capabilities! You're almost there!* Timeless encouraged me again.

Even though I was on the brink of exhaustion, I went on. I spun the electric current, absolutely determined that I'd rather die than quit. When I felt that with my entire being, everything suddenly stopped. Naia's sensor stopped receiving the signal and the robot shot down. Like the signal wasn't even there.

*Nice,* Timeless praised me. *Now be quick, before she wakes up.*

I sat in Naia's body and repeated the connection procedure. Since I got used to the condition of her body the day before, everything went much smoother this time. I didn't trip or stagger anymore. But Timeless did warn me about one more detail.

*Yesterday your perception of reality changed. Soon you were able to sense only the material world. Today try to keep your eyes open for both worlds. So you don't lose me. Use Naia's and your own sight.*

*All right,* I said.

*Now I have a surprise for you,* she said formally. *Follow me.*

I followed her and there was a shining metallic platform waiting for me behind a bush. It had a seat and armrests. In the middle of it was a larger laser console shining brightly. It offered a lot of possibilities for directing and commanding the vehicle.

*Wow,* I thought when I saw it. But it was completely clear to me that it'd take years before I learnt to pilot such a thing.

*Nah, nah, don't be such a pessimist,* she said. *You're a robot now, remember? What if you rummaged a bit through your documents…*

I started searching in my memory. I was looking at the platform in front of me that was only slightly bigger than my body and searching in Naia's memory for images that would match operating such a vehicle. Soon I got plenty of matching hits. Among other things I suddenly gained insight into the precise piloting instructions.

*You see, it's not that bad*, she smiled. *And now get yourself up and show me how to be in charge of this thing!*

## XXXVI. A SURPRISE

As I took off the ground, the platform tilted sideways. I quickly stopped the vehicle and my body leaped upwards. For a moment I hung in the air and then managed to catch the console with one hand. I quickly added the other one and tried to level my body with the platform in mid-air. Soon the force of gravity pushed me back into my seat. I was relieved.

*And now try to be a bit more careful if we want Naia to return home alive,* joked Timeless.

Soon she started giving me more specific instructions.

*Straight ahead! Go back! Turn left! Turn right!*

*Turn around by 360 degrees!*

*Upwards, three meters forwards, turn downwards and straighten!*

*Straighten the vehicle, then make a left loop the loop.*

*Stop in mid-air!*

*Go to the end of the park and back!*

As I carried out all these orders, I was getting better and better. At the same time I began noticing surprised looks below me. The beings that had been watching me, were namely witnessing an interesting scene: a robot piloting the platform by herself and evidently taking pleasure in taking the capabilities of the machine to extremes. Such behavior was unusual for robots. Soon I caught the eye of the robots responsible for public order.

A blue-flashing Ska-robot piloting a platform approached me from below. He waved at me.

Even though I wasn't able to get scared in this body, like I was in my own – because I didn't have any organs – I thought of Timeless.

*What do I do now?*

*Nothing. Act like a robot,* she replied lightly.

We stopped. The Ska-robot came to me.

»Hello, Naia.« I forgot that robots were able to recognize each other – based on their casing vibration.

*His name is Exon,* Timeless sent me a thought.

»Hello, Exon,« I tried to reply as robot-style as possible. He fell for it.

»What does this reckless ride mean?« he asked quickly.

»Oh, that...« I looked at my platform. I was lost for an answer.

*Focus, Zyna. You're a robot,* I heard Timeless again.

»I'm a robot,« I repeated after her.

»What's that?« asked Exon.

»I'm a robot,« I repeated again, only louder this time. »Zyna's Ska-robot,« and pointed towards my/Zyna's body sitting on the blanket.

»Zyna is my owner and she asked me to show her a few maneuvers. Evidently I wasn't very successful, because she fell asleep during my demonstration.« This explanation seemed very good and sensible.

*It is,* Timeless encouraged me.

»I see,« smiled Exon. »Then you can go back to her. She obviously isn't enjoying herself as much as she thought she would.«

»That's true. Yes. Obviously.« I kept imitating robot talk as best as I could.

»Have a nice day. And – be careful with that platform.«

»Okay. Thank you.« I was relieved when he left.

*Where are we going to practice now?* I thought as he left.

*There's no need. Soon you'll be ready. As far as the practice is concerned, I think you're doing just fine. Now it's time for us to lay low again. We've had quite enough of attention.*

When we finished practicing we erased Naia's memory. As I was walking home in my own body accompanied by my robot, I could hardly wait for the next day since Kairon was going to join us again.

## XXXVII. MILITARY STRATEGY

THE NEXT DAY WE MET IN OUR HOUSE. The cameras in my room were luckily gone. Besides, all three of us were present as souls. Nobody could see us.

After the run with Naia, I made an excuse that I was feeling ill and wanted to sleep. I went to my room and lay on the bed. Technically I wasn't lying: when I left my body it did go to sleep, in a way. I knew there was no need to lock my door – should anyone enter the room, they'd be assured I was asleep. Besides, they'd probably become alarmed immediately if they found the door locked: they'd wonder what I was doing in the room.

Timeless and Kairon were extremely punctual. After Kairon and me said hello and hugged, Timeless was ready to start the meeting. She asked us to sit down.

When we obligingly complied with her request, she began her explanation.

»The time is approaching for us to embark on a journey. The knowledge you've been practicing so far will have to be used in real life. And that may not be as pleasant as it was during the practice.«

I remembered certain chips from the library that had an action feel to them and thought it was pretty heroic that I might be a part of such a story.

»Well, on a chip such a story might seem attractive, but in real life you'll need a great deal of concentration for the adventure that awaits you. Do you remember what it took to deactivate the robot?«

We looked at each other. Obviously we've both had problems with it.

»Yes.«

»Multiply that concentration by ten and you'll get a rough idea what I'm talking about.«

»Does that mean we'll have to deactivate ten robots at once?« I asked.

»That means you'll have to improvise,« she explained. »And what's most important, we don't have much time anymore.«

»Why not?« asked Kairon.

»Do you remember what planet Kanter is for?« she asked almost reproachfully.

»Memory deletion.«

»That's right. When a person's memory is deleted, you can try to convince them as much as you want, and they still won't believe you. As long as at least small gaps exist, like in your case Zyna, their condition might still be reversible. That's why we have to hurry over there as quickly as possible. Derek is about to be... deleted.«

I could feel that the matter was really urgent.

»How are we going to travel?« I asked. »By rocket?«

»No, by a couple of platforms,« she answered.

»Platforms?« Kairon was dumbfounded. »But our bodies need oxygen...«

»Who said anything about traveling in your bodies?« smiled Timeless. »Why do you think we've been practicing on robots? For fun?«

That made a lot of sense. The robot's body was much more durable.

»But that planet is light years away from ours.«

»That's why we got together today. So I can explain the schedule to you,« she joked, »or should I say: the law of wormholes!«

# XXXVIII. THE LAW OF WORMHOLES

TIMELESS ASKED US TO CONCENTRATE EVEN MORE. Using the images in her consciousness, she showed us the map and connections between the six planets. They were connected with tunnels. One tunnel led into emptiness.

»This is where planet Earth used to be,« she explained. Then she showed us a simple map that in reality contained a huge part of the universe.

»This is the rest of the planets. They are connected. Other life-containing planets exist too, but they have different codes and connections.« Then she pointed to the map and listed the planets from top to bottom. »The planets interesting to us are: Galactica, Airon, Lunar, Pteor and Kanter. We're heading for the last one.«

»What are the distances between them?« Kairon wanted to know.

»The distance between Skatur and Kanter is six trillion light years.«

I calculated in my head how many million that was. The number seemed unimaginably large.

»And it is,« smiled Timeless. »That's why it's not important what the distance is. It's important how you get there.«

I started to understand her less and less.

»To make a long story short: it's important to be familiar with the wormholes,« she pointed again to the connections between the planets.

»Wormholes are special passages whose functioning is known only to rare beings. Many believe such passages don't even exist. And then there are beings that know about them, but don't have the access to use them. Such traversing namely bestows enormous power that many would abuse.«

»How?« I wanted to know.

»There are numerous possibilities. If somebody sent the inhabitants of planet Airon, which is very cold, to planet Galactica, the entire race could be annihilated. In this way they'd acquire the entire planet and its resources, which are abundant. Whoever would own planet Lunar, which connects all the other planets, could govern all six of them...«

»Oh, now I understand.«

»That's why whoever receives the power to travel through the wormholes must use it solely for good purposes. The Rulers, i.e. the inhabitants of planet Galactica, are obliged to scan any soul that is given the opportunity to acquire this knowledge. This is what awaits the two of you today.«

»Scanning...? Of the soul?«

»Aha,« she smiled again when she noticed the looks on our faces.

»Don't worry. The procedure is completely painless. All you need to do is to remain calm while the Rulers take care of everything else.«

»Where are they?« asked Kairon.

Even before he finished his question, a circle of completely white, glimmering beings formed around us. Although they were different from us – more elongated and somewhat taller – we immediately sensed their joy and some sort of deep-seated happiness.

## XXXIX. THE INITIATION

TIMELESS GAVE US THE FOLLOWING INSTRUCTIONS. *Close your eyes!*
We closed our eyes and tried to relax. I had a hard time following
her instructions, because being curious, I simply had to know what was
going on while I was waiting to be »scanned«. I heard laughter.

*All right, then open them*, said Timeless and I saw that she got their approval.

We sat in the center of the circle, surrounded by white beings. If I
wasn't used to the diversity of beings that was characteristic for our planet,
I'd probably be scared of them. They had glimmering white scales covering
their entire bodies. I could sense that these bodies were faster and much
more powerful than the body of any robot.

They still stood in the circle and they raised their hands. That didn't
seem unusual at all. Then I noticed some sort of a laser connection between their fingers. Like the entire circle held up a straight white thread.
This thread soon turned into a transparent white platform that connected
the hands of everybody participating in the circle. At the same time this
platform represented some sort of roof for Kairon and me.

The Rulers began lowering their hands and the shining platform began
coming down as well. Soon it was just above our heads. I instinctively
closed my eyes. I felt a slight tingling sensation in my head that started
spreading downwards. Soon a strong and very fast vibration engulfed my
entire body. But I couldn't deny feeling pleasantly in it. It was different
from anything else I had experienced until then. I was filled with desire to
move, breathe quickly and run. Even though as a soul I didn't need oxygen.

The vibration rose and lowered a few more times. Then it accumulated in Kairon and me. It was becoming faster and faster, and I could feel that I might stand it more easily as a robot. Soon it began losing its intensity; it started disappearing inside our bodies. When it completely disappeared I opened my eyes again and noticed that the Rulers were smiling. They were still in a circle, only now they were sitting.

*You have our blessing,* said the tallest one. *Aside from being curious from time to time, there are no evil thoughts or intentions in you. Since your souls are pure and young, they represent a strong foundation for the completion of your task. Good luck.*

The beings stood up again and each of them placed their hand on us. Again I felt a strong and fast vibration that shot like electricity through me. *I'll have to get used to that,* I thought.

*There'll be plenty of time for that,* answered the main Ruler. Soon they disappeared in their characteristic quick frequency and we were alone again.

## XL. THE PARTING

THE NEXT DAY TIMELESS GAVE US CLEAR INSTRUCTIONS: »You should appear to be more and more tired and if anybody asks you anything, say that you're very sleepy!«

I understood. It was a part of the plan. If we managed to convince our parents and the others around us that we were coming down with the sleeping sickness, our bodies could seemingly stay asleep for several days. In the meantime we could complete our task without any difficulties in the bodies of robots.

On the day of departure I was thoroughly prepared. I kept asking Naia to keep me company. Mom was thrilled at the thought that we became so close.

At the appointed time I was lying in bed and Naia was sitting next to me. I left my body and found myself behind the nape of her neck. As I demagnetized her, I was grateful that Timeless made me practice this so many times. It went easier than I had expected. Or the signal was somewhat weaker that day.

Again in the robot's body I looked at my own body. I automatically took the hand of the sleeping body and said: »Hang on, I'll be back soon.«

In the meantime Timeless also started to participate in the plan. She rang our doorbell and my mom opened the front door.

»Hello! I've been sent by Nox civic authorities. Does Ska-robot Naia work for you?«

»Yes, of course,« said mom, who hadn't experienced something like that before.

»A new protocol, madam,« Timeless said officially. »In the interest of your safety, we've organized a compulsory robot checkup, to be performed once a year. Naia will have to come with me for a few days.«

»A few days? Oh my. My daughter is recuperating from the sleeping disease, you know, and Naia's at her side right now. She's of great assistance to her. Couldn't you come back in a few days...?«

»I'm sorry madam, but that's procedure. Maybe you could stay at your daughter's side, if she really needs the company. But if she's sleeping, then it probably doesn't make a difference anyway.«

»Well, all right. Wait here and I'll go and get her,« said mom.

I quickly sat next to my bed again and prepared to play my role.

»Naia?« she said as she came to the room.

I turned my head towards her robot-like. »Yes?«

»The checkup... I mean, you have to answer the door because you're getting a checkup.«

»I know. I just received the message,« I was trying to be as convincing as possible. To stress the importance of the situation I was holding one hand to my temple like I really received the message.

»The repair lady is waiting for you downstairs.«

»Excellent,« I said and stood up. »Be well, Zyna,« I waved at my body.

When I saw Timeless, I almost started to laugh. Everything went much smoother than I thought it would.

*Be patient, we're not on planet Kanter yet,* she warned me. Since my mom was watching us go, we had to walk the way our roles demanded for quite some time. Me as a robot and Timeless as my repair lady.

*Nice hat,* I thought when we got far enough.

*As befits a repair lady,* she joked. Soon she grew solemn again thinking about our plan.

*Come on, Kairon's already waiting.*

## XLI. THE JOURNEY

**K**AIRON WAS WAITING FOR US IN HRYLON PARK, IN GAI'S BODY.
»Nice casing, Zyna,« he waved at me.

»I could say the same for you, Kai,« I replied. Timeless interrupted us again.

*The park is equipped with cameras too. Be careful with your real names. You're Naia and Gai at the moment.*

*Right*, we thought simultaneously.

There were a couple of platforms parked next to Kairon: a bigger and a smaller one.

*The smaller one's for you, Zyna*, thought Timeless. *It'll be easier for you to enter the storage space. The bigger one's for the three of us.*

*Three?*

*Me, Kairon and Derek.*

*Oh, right.*

*And remember: the more the vibration of your bodies changes, the more you need to relax. Regardless of how much you may want to obey the reflexes of the metal you're wearing.*

*Right*, we thought again.

As we took to the sky I was overwhelmed by the feeling of importance. *This is it*, I thought.

*Look straight ahead, Zyna*, Timeless responded. *Follow us!*

Soon I noticed the town of Nox below me and realized that I'd never flown so high up on the platform. If I wanted to fly that high in my own body I'd need a space suit. *Did we take a spare space suit for Derek?* I wanted to know. *Don't worry, the complete equipment is in here,* Timeless assured me and pointed to the baggage compartment on the bigger platform.

After a while, we noticed that there was a storm coming on. The clouds started to whirl in a strange way.

*That's not a storm,* Timeless thought. *That's the portal through which we're about to travel. My thought frequency has connected with the administrator of the planet Lunar and he's opened a wormhole for us. We must hurry. Full speed ahead!* she instructed us and then they vanished in the tunnel in front of me. I too rushed into it and got sucked in faster than I expected.

*Hold on to your console,* I heard her voice in my head, *otherwise relax. Don't control the machine, because it doesn't work in this vibration anyway. Close your eyes!*

I closed my eyes which were already tired from the whirling. After a few seconds of slight trembling I realized that my body started to vibrate faster than the electric current that flowed through my wires. I hoped that my body wouldn't demagnetize…

*This is what I've been talking about,* Timeless warned us. *Relax your wires and the entire system. Surrender to the undulation…*

Soon afterwards I sensed sudden peace. The vibrating had stopped and I felt like I was swimming in a timeless space. A voice woke me from the dream:

*Zyna, hold your vehicle!*

I realized that we already left the wormhole. In front of us we saw a dark planet whose surface seemed metallic and wrinkled from afar. I held on to my platform that almost got away from me and followed Kairon and Timeless. The magnetic field of this planet was much stronger than the one on Skatur and I could feel being pulled towards the surface much stronger that usual.

*Adjust your vehicle,* I heard the new instruction. *Look through your data*

*for how to pilot on planet Kanter.*

I focused and quickly found what I was looking for. My only problem was that I often forgot that I already had the answers to my problems and that I just needed to browse through my files to find them.

Since Kanter was a bigger planet than Skatur, I needed more power to drive normally. Thanks to Timeless, the vehicles were prepared very well.

When we got closer to the wrinkled surface, I noticed that it was covered with some sort of red light grid.

*These are the lasers we have to avoid,* she warned us.

We got to the surface and landed on one of the brown protrusions. The distance between the individual laser beams in the grid was big enough for me to drive through without a problem. As I looked around I was faced with not exactly an idyllic scene...

## XLII. THE DEPOSITORY

THE BROWN WRINKLED METALLIC PROTRUSIONS OBVIOUSLY FORMED some sort of a roof.

*Soon you'll see what this is,* Timeless told us when we parked. Each protrusion had a handle on one side. Timeless grabbed one of them and opened the hatch. This depository obviously had doors on every step!

*There are so many doors because there are so many species. If somebody wants to access a certain species, all they have to do is know where that species is on the map.*

*We'll have to leave elsewhere though,* she warned us.

*Once we open Derek's coffin all the roof doors will close. Help me bring in the platforms,* she thought.

We barely managed to squeeze the platforms through the entrance.

Inside the depository, we ended up on some sort of a small ledge.

*Activate the platforms again, but very quietly,* Timeless thought.

I found the information in my documents on how to pilot the platform without making a sound. Kairon did the same.

We sat on our vehicles and slowly left the ledge. A completely new world opened to us under the ledge: a deep space full of transparent coffins filled with transparent yellow liquid.

*Zyna, Kairon, find the map of this place.*

Amazingly enough, this turned out to be quite a simple task too. Naia's consciousness really contained a lot of information!

*It's like that with all robots,* answered Timeless. *Stop there!*

She pointed at the ledge above one of the huge docks. We stopped. Kairon and me looked through the maps in the documents belonging to our robots.

*From here on you're going alone,* thought Timeless.

*How is that?* I asked. It seemed impossible to go on without her guidance.

*I'll join you as soon as you complete the task. You'll be less noticeable without me. I have my ways of traveling. I just had to direct you this far. See you outside.*

*We'll stay in touch anyway,* she joked. *Derek's coffin sticks out a bit. I took care of that — so you can find it more easily.*

We sat behind the consoles of our respective platforms again and headed towards the right coffin. We must have come too close to the wall at some point, because something started beeping. Like some sort of alarm. I found the fastest way to get to Derek's coffin on my map. I led the way, checking from time to time if Kairon was still behind me…

*Kairon, turn left!* I quickly shouted in my mind when I saw him getting too close to the big depository. He turned towards me.

*How much time do we have?*

*I don't know, but not too much, I guess!* I quickly answered.

Transparent coffins containing transparent yellow liquid were stacked one atop another and we flew as fast as we could.

*Look, over here!* I pointed with my finger. It was as our mentor had said — one of the coffins actually stuck out of the pile.

We got closer and looked inside. A young boy with black hair, thin lips and somewhat square face was resting in the liquid. In that moment my memory became crystal clear. Above the coffin was an indicator saying:

»Deleted: 95%«.

*Oh, no, we have to hurry up!* I moaned.

Kairon took hold of the coffin's bottom part and grasped a couple of handles. He pulled one out and pushed the other in. The lid opened up and I reached my hand into the liquid.

The boy had an electrode attached to his head. It was fitted with a needle that was stuck into his brain. I pressed the pin and the electrode opened up. I took the needle out. In that exact moment an even louder alarm sounded. The boy opened his eyes. I handed him a towel, fresh clothes and an oxygen helmet and helped him put on a spacesuit. When he regained full consciousness he started asking questions.

»What's happened?«

»There's no time for explanations,« I said quickly. »Come with us if you want to live!«

He quickly climbed on Kairon's hovering platform. Despite both of us driving extremely fast, we weren't sure we'd reach the exit in time. We'd been spotted and the door was beginning to close.

*Faster, Zyna!* Kairon encouraged me. He had to turn his platform upright to get through.

»I'm not losing you,« I said to nobody in particular. »It's still possible to get through!« The door in front of me was almost closed when I pressed the acceleration key even harder…

In the next second everything unfolded like in a slow motion. I could see the door closing in front of me and I wasn't fast enough to slip through. When I was quite near the door I made a decision. I closed my eyes and tried to disconnect my soul from Naia's cardiac cluster. In the next moment I heard the sound of a powerful collision and metal being torn to shreds.

Part two
# Derek

WE WERE STANDING IN A CIRCLE. We knew that we had only one shot. Soon we received the last warning from the Rulers:

»Leave, or you won't just die. You'll disintegrate.«

We looked at each other.

»It's all right,« said the leader of the group and looked at me, »If necessary, you know what you have to do. Protect Zyna.«

»And Kairon,« added the blonde.

»And for now: continue.«

I was holding a USB flash drive in front of me. It was small, oval – shaped like a capsule – and barely noticeable. The two couples stepped closer. They raised their hands and sent the contents we talked about into the small device I was holding in my hand. The light that directed itself like a precise laser towards the microscopically small circuit finally found the appropriate space and settled down in the device. The four of them sighed with relief.

»It's done,« I confirmed.

»You're right, it really is *done*!« I heard a hoarse voice behind my back. Without turning around I quickly swallowed the USB flash drive.

»Go now, Derek,« calmly said the blonde. »You're not on our side! There's no place among us for those who yielded to the darkness!« I thought that she could put more effort into dramatizing her words and I wasn't sure that the Darkened would believe her. Luckily I was wrong. I turned around and slowly walked towards the basement.

»You think you're done with us. Unfortunately... you've just begun!« said the hoarse voice. The dark beings scattered around the room and soon I couldn't see anything anymore. Luckily for me they initially left me alone. As we had expected. I closed the door behind me, but it soon started to crack. Horror-stricken I watched how precisely the plan was unfolding. It *really* was pre-arranged for the planet to disintegrate!

Mourning for my friends I ran quickly to save the last treasure I'd been entrusted with: the children.

# I. THE INTERVIEW

I STUCK MY TONGUE INTO MY SAKÉ AND IMMEDIATELY PUT THE CUP back on the tray. The drink that Chinese restaurants typically used to make up for what their food lacked was totally tasteless. I left more than half of the meal I ordered on my plate and that was only because I was starving. I had decided beforehand that I wouldn't cut any slack to anyone. The food stunk.

I waited for a person to question about hygiene. I had noticed some stains on the plate of sweet and sour chicken that I ordered that didn't actually belong there. I could hardly wait for someone to explain to me why this type of restaurant should even be in business in the first place. I couldn't care less that the prices were half of what they were in other restaurants. Restaurants of this standard should be closed down.

"Thank you for visiting The Red Dragon, the traditional family-run restaurant in the center of Tianjin," recited the waitress in a bored voice as I paid my bill while gritting my teeth.

"Actually," I said to her as she was returning my change. Of course I didn't leave any tip at all. "I'm Derek Blake. I'm a journalist and I have an appointment with someone here to show me around the place."

"Oh, sure," said the waitress while changing her tone from totally bored to a little less bored. "She'll be right with you," she smiled kindly.

She went to the counter where she shouted out somebody's name. Chinese names had always sounded so similar to me. There was a joke in high school that Chinese people chose the names for their children by throwing a can down a flight of stairs and listening to the sounds it produced. The women mumbled something in their language and smiled meaningfully a couple of times. A young waitress came up to me and shook my hand.

"I'm Ching Lan. Nice to meet you," she said smiling.

"My name is Derek Blake," I said formally. I wanted to let her know that the interview wasn't going to be exactly pleasant. I expected an explanation of their standards of hygiene and awful food.

"I know that," she replied smiling. I looked up again. Although all Chinese women looked the same to me, this one really might have looked a little more familiar. Where was it that I saw her…?

"Can you refresh my memory…?" I said uncertainly.

"New York. The high school near the Central Park. We were classmates for a year. Derek Blake – the boy who was to write a bestseller!"

Suddenly I became really embarrassed. I couldn't even remember her name while she not only knew who I was but was also able to remember my long-forgotten dreams! I had always wanted to become a writer. I would get an idea and it would become a hit. Great Hollywood films would be made according to my books, I would become a part of the richest and the most influential people in the world… nothing like my father, who was still talking pictures of animals in Africa and writing meaningless articles about safaris. I wanted to be more than that.

After five years of trying to get a great idea and using up all of my savings, I had to admit defeat – I got a job as a journalist writing for a small travel magazine that published unimportant articles about unimportant things. Such as a small earthquake in some Pacific islands. Or types of pets in Scotland. And of course the traditional family Chinese restaurant in the city called Tianjin, south of Beijing. The only thing about my job that I liked was traveling. I received a cheap tourist package in Tianjin and some money to cover my expenses of visiting local tourist attractions.

Suddenly the time I had spent as a journalist seemed utterly demeaning. The person sitting opposite me knew me at the time when I still had my dreams… before I became so totally disappointed with how my life had turned out. There is no wonder that in my own disappointment with my life I would look only for shortcomings in other people and enjoy teaching people, who in my opinion didn't do their work professionally, a lesson. Not only that my witty ironic insults would entertain my readers; they also brought me some short-term satisfaction. I had managed to find people who were even *less successful* than me. So I could make fun of *them*. I intended to do the same about the restaurant I was sitting in. Up until the moment when my ex-schoolmate pushed me to the point when I had to face what I used to be. I cannot even begin to describe my embarrassment. I felt totally disarmed.

And I knew absolutely nothing about her. I had always hung out with people who had a similar sized ego to my own. I thought it cool to write lyrics for our class band and imagined them to become hits one day. I used to contribute to the school newsletter and pretended I was writing a chapter of one of my novels. And later when I finished first high school and then university and moved, I saw myself as one of the major attractions at parties where people discussed my works that had received numerous literary prizes and everybody had read…

I always sought out people that looked important. I never mixed with ordinary people like the woman sitting next to me now. She had always been a timid sort and she didn't draw attention to herself. Now I suddenly felt sorry for making fun of Chinese names. I would have done anything to be able to greet her with her name… What was it again – Chong Lang, Chao Long, Chin Lin…?

"Oh my God, I can't believe it!" I heard myself say feeling sincerely happy and embarrassed at the same time.

"I'm really sorry, it's been ages… Hello, my dear schoolmate…?" I offered to shake hands again.

"Ching Lan," she introduced herself again and smiled. "I know it's hard for westerners to remember our names… Like listening to a can falling down a flight of stairs or something," she said remembering the joke from high school years.

I felt embarrassed again. *I will never make fun of Chinese names again,* I thought humbly while fervently repeating the two syllables that were her name: Ching Lan, Ching Lan, Ching Lan...

"Ching Lan, of course," I said trying to sound relaxed. "I spent only a year at that school and the names of my classmates are a bit blurry, I'm afraid to say."

"That's OK," she replied. "You're here to write about our family restaurant, right?" she said changing the subject. I was embarrassed again.

"Actually, yes." Since she had managed to reopen the wounds from my past, I decided to write about this restaurant as objectively as I possibly could. If I wasn't able to write in superlatives about the food they served, I could maybe focus on the long tradition and history.

"How long has this restaurant been in your family?" I asked with real interest.

"Well, for quite a long time, actually. One hundred and fifty years."

"That's a long tradition," I said with a smile. I could feel sweat running down my back and I realized I was very nervous.

"Do you have any specialty that you would recommend to the readers of this magazine?" I asked trying to sound objective.

"Ants Creeping up a Tree," she replied with a bored voice. "But usually people order something not too unusual. Like sweet and sour chicken or fish."

"And... I mean your parents... Your family... Has your family been in this business all this time?" I started running out of questions. Before she came I had a total plan worked out how I was going to humiliate her completely. Little did I know that it was going to be the other way around.

"Yes, my parents, too, sure," she said sounding relaxed. She looked at me as if she wanted to ask me something serious.

"Can I ask you something?" she said.

"Sure thing, go ahead," I said putting down my notepad.

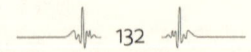

"Did you enjoy the food?" she asked smiling.

"Oh, yes, sure. Well, people have different tastes, you know. This is Chinese tradition," I tried to talk my way out of it while feeling a waterfall running down my back.

"I don't like it either. Actually, I find it quite disgusting," she replied now laughing out loud.

"Really? And why do you…?"

"Work here? That's a long story. Fancy a walk?" she asked relaxed. I couldn't say no to her. And I could hardly wait to escape from that stinking place. Even if I made a fool out of myself in her company again.

"Sure. With pleasure," I said and I felt that she was truly happy I accepted her invitation. I finished my glass of water which turned out to be the only consumable thing I had been served that day.

I took my coat and Ching Lan quickly said goodbye to her friend. They laughed at some verbal joke again – told in Chinese, of course. And then she joined me. Her black hair was arranged in a ponytail and she put a cap on her head since it was pretty cold outside.

"Shall we have some real food?" she smiled. "It's my treat."

## II. GORGEOUS ORCHID

"CHING LAN?" I said turning to her.

"So you can remember better. My name means gorgeous orchid," she said smiling and pointed at her body. "If you hadn't been reminded of a stem with leaves up to now, you sure will be from now on!"

"Not really. I mean not in that sense. You are really pretty," I kept babbling realizing that maybe I was being a bit to direct. "I mean, pretty as an orchid."

"Well, thank you," she said and turned around again. It was late afternoon and we were walking along a street. I found it interesting seeing how many different types of vehicles there were on the street. Many of those would never be allowed to drive in the yard and much less in the street back home. You could see combinations of handcarts and motorbikes, bikes and luggage racks, cars and three-wheelers.

"Observing the traffic, are you?" she asked.

"Yes."

"Very creative, don't you think?"

I was surprised how she seemed to have been able to read my mind all afternoon.

"Well, I don't know…"

"Well, in Britain and America they would never be allowed to drive in the street," she said and smiled. I was disarmed again. When I realized that any pretense fails in her presence, I decided to put all the games I usually played with girls to the side. Before I could change my mind, I blurted: "Ching Lan?"

"Yes?"

"I'm sorry."

"For what?" she was curious.

"When I was at the restaurant I wanted…"

"Embarrass the owners? That's quite all right. I would have probably tried to do the same thing if I were you," she concluded again.

"But that wasnt't right."

"It doesn't matter. The atmosphere is gloomy, the light is poor, the music is always the same and most importantly: the food is inedible. I still want you to write that."

"Well, I don't want that anymore…"

"What were you suppose to write?"

"The article was suppose to be about tradition… Maybe I won't write about your restaurant at all. To protect you," I tried to remedy the situation.

"Well, yes, maybe."

We turned right towards a bigger street that looked like a market place. People were shopping for T-shirts, souvenirs, shells and statuettes.

"We are sure to find something delicious here," she said and smiled.

"Here?"

"In Tianjin it usually happens that you find good things where you least expect them," she concluded and pointed to a stall with some sort of meat skewers.

"What do you fancy? I'll have the salmon."

"Can I have the same, please?" I asked. Considering the fact that we agreed about their restaurant I was hoping it would be the same here. The guy at the grill served us two huge portions and added a couple of pieces of a special kind of bread.

"Tradition," smiled Ching Lan. "Like fish and chips in England."

I smiled back. I was being rendered utterly speechless the whole evening. She could have said anything to me and I would have been completely unable to form a witty answer. But still I felt somehow... young in her company. I felt happy.

We walked past different stalls and ate our food, which was truly delicious.

"This is really great," I blurted while stuffing my face with a fantastic fish skewer.

"I told you I would take you to try some real food," she said and smiled.

We ate in silence for a while. If this is what you called the hustle and bustle surrounding us. When we were done, Ching Lan took the paper plates to the garbage bin. We continued walking among the stalls. You could really buy anything – fabric, T- shirts, paintings... We saw another stall with food. There was a big red poster with a picture of something that resembled a soufflé, and many Chinese characters. But not a word in English.

"I won't translate that for you, all I can tell you is that it's a sweet," she said mysteriously.

"OK, but this is on me," I added quickly.

"OK. But you are eating this at your own risk," she went on.

She said something to the vendor – in Chinese of course – and both of them laughed. When I looked at her questioningly, she said: "You look like you've just been sentenced to death."

"Well, I'm not exactly sure what I'm getting myself into, that's all," I replied trying to maintain my dignity.

I was mostly observing all the ingredients the confectioner needed to prepare his product: many different ingredients that I didn't even recognize. There was also something that looked like a big golden teakettle with tassels on its stand; I had no idea what was in it. When he was preparing our portions, he mixed all the ingredients together and in the end he poured some of the warm liquid from the kettle over them. He mixed it all together and gave the bowls to us. I paid and we set off again.

"You go first," she said and gestured towards my bowl.

I took the spoon and put it in the bowl. When I put it into my mouth, I was utterly amazed: the sweet concoction of all imaginable ingredients – maybe hazel nuts, some other nuts and rum – it gave me an intoxicating feeling I had no name for. It spread around my tongue and created a delicious symphony of intermingling tastes. For the first time in my life, I tingled all over my body. I had never eaten anything that fantastic. "Oh, my God," I sighed when I swallowed my first bite.

"Do you like it?" she asked feeling proud.

"Like? I'm in love," I said honestly.

"Great. The recipe is traditional but I was the one who suggested a secret ingredient. And since that time, his stall is always busy. We went to elementary school together, you know."

"Did you?" I didn't know why I suddenly became jealous. *Get a grip, Derek. You don't even know the girl.*

"What's with the tone? You're not jealous, are you?"

I started to sweat again. It sounded like a joke coming from her mouth but the fact was that she had just read me like an open book. I had to do something to get out of this.

"I'm jealous of the recipe. I would become rich if I had it," I tried. Soon we arrived at a bridge dominated by the presence of a big Ferris wheel.

"The Tianjin Eye," Ching Lan explained. "Do you fancy a ride? I know the manager."

"Well, if I can get in without having to pay for it, then I won't say no," I said joking. I wanted to sound witty but I had a feeling that all my effort was completely wasted. I felt totally small and insignificant in her company.

When we finished our desserts, she went up to the counter and said something in Chinese again. The woman at the counter smiled and then escorted us to the capsule.

"Do people always smile here when they talk to someone?"

"Well, I have never thought about that," she said. "But I guess you are right."

The door closed and we started moving slowly. We were alone but I noticed some guides that explained how far and what we could see.

"I could explain the view to you but I guess you will forget about that sooner or later," she said. "And it's not even that important."

I looked at her. The sun had already started to set and in the orange light her immaculate complexion glowed even more. Her full lips, to which she must have just applied something, glittered seductively while her huge eyes suddenly looked directly at me. I quickly averted my gaze in embarrassment because she had just caught me again.

"Do you want to know why I work in that restaurant?" she asked me.

"Yes, sure," I said interested.

"As a matter of fact, I used to have big dreams too. I trained kung fu. Soon after finishing high school I intended to take part in one of the biggest competitions. But it was already in the semi-finals that I received an illegal kick to my knee. And that's how my career came to an end."

"Just like that?" I couldn't believe that one's dreams can be shattered so quickly after years of working so hard.

"Well, if the blow is strong enough, then yes, just like that. The girl was disqualified immediately but that didn't help me much. I tried to return each year but I couldn't. At the same time I completed my studies of languages in New York. I studied English, Chinese, Japanese and French. I was prepared to do just about anything just so that I wouldn't have to go back home. But I guess language teachers were not in great demand. And then my mom, who had run the restaurant business, died. The food used to be much better because she really had a knack for this business. I inherited the place because it has been in the family for so long. After years of trying to make it in New York I had to admit defeat and return back home. And because I wasn't brave enough to sell the place – there were many arguments about family inheritance – I stayed here. And the food here is no better than my life…" she smiled bitterly.

I was amazed how similar her life story was to mine. I would have done anything to keep her from suffering. And again I blurted something that made no sense at all.

"Why don't you come live with me?"

"What?"

"To London."

"Do you need a flatmate to share expenses with?" she said joking.

"Well, not really."

"Why then?" she asked me questioningly.

"Oh, nothing. Forget it," I tried to cover up my confusion. I really didn't know what to think about her. No woman had ever before made me feel so... familiar. I really wanted to live with her – I could find no explanation for that feeling. She made me be who I really was. Just Derek. Without my platitudes and philosophizing. She was the only one that made me take off my mask.

"We've reached the top!" she said.

"Sorry, what?"

"Look!"

I looked out and the view was absolutely breathtaking. The river flowing under the bridge sparkled in the setting sun and I noticed that the city lights started switching on. As she was standing next to me I felt her presence even stronger. Feeling nervous I gently put my hand on her shoulder.

"Derek," she said quietly. "This won't work."

"Why not?"

"Because I'm here and you're there," she said quickly.

"And besides, you are not the type for a family restaurant. You wouldn't fit in with my sisters and my father."

"You don't fit either. I can take you away from here," I said persistently.

"You barely know me!" she tried to reason.

She was right about that. I didn't know her but at the same time I had the feeling I knew her much longer than it seemed at the first glance.

"You're right. I don't know you."

I moved back. Our journey was coming to an end. I was surprised how the day had turned out. This afternoon I was totally ready to make somebody's life miserable. And by the end of the evening I was… sort of in love. I wanted to be with her and I couldn't even explain it to myself. She just seemed so similar to me, so complementary, so gentle and beautiful that life without her would be totally pointless. I decided to insist. When we reached firm ground again we continued walking in silence.

"I should go back," she said. It sounded like an apology.

"OK."

"How long are you staying…?"

"Two more days."

"Right," she said. I knew she wasn't totally indifferent either. She was struggling with herself about what to do. Should she trust a stranger and devote two days of her life to him? Just like that? Despite the consequences?

"I'll come again tomorrow," I insisted.

"If you enjoy eating bad food, go ahead," she smiled.

"Not really. But I'm enjoying spending time with you."

And before she could reply we reached the Red Dragon. She waved and disappeared behind the door.

## III. THE NEXT DAY

I RAN AROUND THE ROOM LIKE CRAZY LOOKING FOR A SUITABLE SHIRT. The white one with blue stripes was the only one that really suited me. When I couldn't find it I was sure it had been stolen. I ran to the reception desk where a friendly-looking receptionist greeted me.

"Good morning. Do you happen to know where my shirt is? The white one with blue stripes – checked?"

She looked at me and said some indistinct words in Chinese or rather in the Tianjin dialect.

"Shirt," I said and pointed to my torso to make her understand me better.

"It was in my room yesterday," I explained and gestured wildly with my hands.

Her answer remained the same. I took off my shirt and pointed at it.

"Shirt, shirt!" I kept repeating and pointing at it.

"Shirt," she repeated after me with a Chinese accent. "Yes, yes, shirt! Here," she said and motioned for me to follow her.

I followed her past the kitchen to a tiny little room that resembled a laundry room. I could see my shirt in one of the washing machines.

"But it was clean!" I started to argue.

"Shirt, floor, wash," said the receptionist.

I remembered the hotel rules. If you leave something on the floor, you want to have it washed. And here they took that seriously. I must have dropped it by mistake. And now that it was being washed, it was way too late to rescue it and wear it to my date.

"When?" I asked pointing first at my watch and then the shirt.

"To-morrow," said the receptionist pointing her finger upwards trying

to let me know that was in the future.

"Oh, no," I whined. When I saw there was nothing she could do about it I went back to my room. "Thank you. Goodbye," I said waving my hand so she would understand me. Back in my room, I went through my miserable wardrobe one more time.

I had packed a red shirt, since I was going to China, and now I saw I looked like a waiter from the Red Dragon in it. I also had a shirt I had worn the previous day.

I suppose there is no other way, I thought to myself when I was putting on the red horror. Next time I was definitely packing everything I owned.

Ching Lan had agreed to go to the cinema with me that day. There was a romantic film on that her friend had seen and liked. She told me on the phone that she was getting off at four. We could have something to eat first and then go to the cinema... At the very thought that I was to spend the evening with her I felt more alive than ever before. No woman had ever turned my head as she did in just a couple of hours. I was surprised to realize how euphoric I felt when I was choosing the shoes to go with that terrible shirt.

*It's just a date*, I kept saying to myself. And at the same time I was completely out of my mind with excitement.

At half past three I looked at myself in the mirror hoping I didn't look too posh for going to the cinema. I was absolutely clueless about Chinese dating habits and dress code.

I called a taxi and at five to four I was standing in front of her restaurant with a bunch of flowers in my hands.

She came out smiling and seeing me with flowers made her laugh out loud. I guessed my red shirt peeking out from under my jacket also contributed to her laughter.

"What's wrong?" I asked unsure of myself.

"Nothing. It's you," she said pointing at me. "You've spruced up really nicely."

She looked great too. She wore a skirt and there was a little bit more make up on her eyes. I guessed I wasn't completely off then. She took care of her appearance too.

"You look… very beautiful," I said hesitantly and offered her the flowers. I felt like a second grader.

"Oh, thank you," she said. "Would you mind if I put them in a vase here…?"

"No, not at all," I agreed. That was the best thing to do. I didn't know why I had decided to bring her flowers. How did I imagine the evening to develop? She couldn't carry them around all night. How unpractical.

When she came back from the restaurant – I could see the flowers on the main bar – we went to eat. Since I couldn't afford a limo, I chose one of the city taxis. And I was very embarrassed. The taxi driver kept speaking on the phone, which annoyed me extremely. Ching Lan smiled.

"He's got family problems," she said to me quietly. "He's talking to his wife."

"Really?" I became interested.

"Yes. And he doesn't like taking us out to a restaurant when he and his wife haven't eaten out for a very long time."

"Now you're making it up," I said and looked at her sideways.

She laughed. "I just wanted to put you in a better mood. I hope that a man speaking on the phone is not going to ruin our evening!"

She was right again. This time we went to a restaurant the hotel receptionist had recommended. He started work at 1 p.m. and he even spoke English.

"If the girl is a native of Tianjin, do not take her to a traditional Tianjin restaurant but choose a European or an American restaurant," he advised me. "The locals have different interests than tourists."

And so we arrived at "Island Bar & Grill."

"I hear they serve a mean chimichanga here," I said wanting to impress her.

"Let's see," she said mysteriously.
"Have you eaten here before…?"

"No, not yet. Have you?" she smiled.

"I eat here every day," I replied.

When we sat down the atmosphere became a bit more relaxed. We

ordered and then she started to look around the room. I was really glad I managed to surprise her. For once she hadn't been able to read everything that was going on in my mind.

"Ching Lan," I started. "I'd like to apologize for my behavior yesterday."

"Don't worry about it," she replied. "I behaved pretty... irresponsibly myself."

"What do you mean?"

"If I had been responsible and smart, I wouldn't have fallen in lo..."

"Two times chimichanga with black beans and rice, please!" the waitress announced and interrupted us.

She put the trays and the drinks in front of us smiling and then asked us if we needed anything else. But I couldn't care less about the food that was just served.

Ching Lan dove into her food. "Enjoy the food."

When she swallowed her first bite, she turned to me. "The food is absolutely delicious. Aren't you hungry?"

"I'm waiting for you to continue your sentence that you started a minute ago," I replied. "And then I will eat. Only then I'll be able to breathe again."

"Then consider this a test of how long you can hold your breath," she joked and put a full fork of her food in her mouth.

"Oh, come on," I begged her. "What did you want to tell me?"

"I wanted to say the food was really delicious!"

"Before that!"

"I wished you to enjoy your food..."

"Before – that!"

She looked down. "I wanted to say that I... cared too."

"Cared about what?"

"You."

I pricked up my ears, but Ching Lan started eating quickly again. I stopped her.

"I'd like to know a little more, please."

"There's nothing to say. The food is really good..." But I noticed that her eyes became a little moist. I put down my fork.

"What's the matter, Ching Lan?"

"I don't want to spoil our evening. Can we just eat, please?"

I picked up my fork and started to eat. I noticed that the food was really very good and at the same time I kept looking in her direction. She was eating very fast and I could see that every now and again a tear would drop into her plate. I had no idea why.

That was more or less everything I could think about while we ate. I barely noticed the smiling waitresses and the pretty good background music. My love was sad and I had no idea why. When we finished our meal I paid the bill quickly and then we went for a walk. When we walked towards the cinema, I held her hand.

"Can you just let it go, please?" she said with calmness in her voice.

"Why?" I asked her and made my grip firmer.

"Because you've decided to hold my hand five years too late, OK?" she said a bit louder and managed to wriggle her hand out of my grip. "There is something I must tell you!"

"Please go ahead!"

"I used to have a crush on you, Derek."

I didn't know what she meant.

"In high school. You were so... smart and you radiated some kind of vivaciousness. You were different than everybody else. I wanted to talk to you so many times, but you just didn't notice me... I imagined what we could do together. We could go to concerts, dates; we could stay there in New York. I looked forward to the new term during the whole summer break. And then... you disappeared."

"Ching Lan..."

"Forget it. That's ancient history."

"Ching Lan," I tried again. I was deeply moved. "I was too full of myself at that time to notice anybody. But now I can *see* you. And I like you tremendously."

We stopped and I cupped her tear-stained face with my hands. I decided to take a risk and try to move it closer to me. She closed her eyes.

She looked so beautiful under streetlights. I didn't want to take any risks so I put my lips on hers. They were so soft… I felt I wanted to be with her. No matter what.

"But you're leaving the day after tomorrow," she said when she got over from her surprise.

"Yes, that's right," I replied. "But I can come back, if your grace should wish that," I said dramatically and curtsied.

She smiled through her tears.

"And then, what will you do then?"

"Then I will kidnap you and take you to America. And we will go to all the concerts we missed five years ago. Then we will live together, we will start a family and live happily to the day we die," I recapped. "Am I being too concrete?"

"No… that's OK. If you really… come back…"

"I promise I will!" I said firmly and hugged her. I lifted her up and swung her around and I could feel she was happy. We were so preoccupied with ourselves that we almost forgot about the film.

"Oh, what about the film?" she remembered. "We've missed it!"

"We've just witnessed our own private romcom, don't you think?" I said and smiled. "The girl who hooks up with her high school crush…"

"You're right," she added.

I walked her home. She lived close by. Too close. We agreed I should come to pick her up the next day.

*I hope the shirt with blue stripes will be dry by then*, I thought before we said goodbye. Halfway to my taxi I turned around and saw that she was still looking at me. I went back and hugged her again. I don't remember how many goodnight kisses I gave her. But when I was going back to my hotel I still thought not enough.

## IV. GOODBYE

WE WERE LEANING AGAINST THE TAXI DOOR HOLDING EACH OTHER in a firm embrace.

"Don't go," she whispered in my ear. "I'll arrange everything for you, visa, residence permit, whatever you want, just don't go," she implored me. I didn't want to leave her either but I knew I had to. I had decided firmly to return the following week.

"I'll be back next week," I promised her. "I have a surprise for you."

This statement put her in a better mood. "Really?"

"Yes, really."

I hugged her one more time trying to soak up the sweet smell of her hair and skin. How was it possible that I hadn't noticed her in the whole year we spent going to the same school when she was so beautiful?

I was running late for my flight so I had to say goodbye quickly.

"You're right. Just go. Who needs you," she said joking.

I sat into my taxi and opened the back window.

"If you fail to show up in a week's time, I'll find myself a boyfriend," she threatened jokingly.

"I'll be back, honey. You just make sure you are ready to leave." She glowed like no one else.

"If you really think…"

"Really."

The taxi pulled off and I blew her a kiss. When we turned the first corner I thought that I might have been too cheesy. Blowing kisses seemed

a bit immature considering how real the love I felt for her was. I could hardly wait to return. Ching Lan gave me all the addresses and phone numbers – the restaurant's as well as her home. And of course the only thing I could think about at the airport was her.

My flight home dragged like never before. It rained at the airport so my flight was postponed by half an hour. The selection of movies available didn't impress me and when I started playing with my mobile the flight attendant was quick to inform me that the use of mobiles was not permitted. So the only thing I could do was lean back in my seat and start making plans about what I would do when I arrived home.

I had managed to save some money in this year since I had a paying job. Maybe I could even apply for a loan or something. And then I would put away the burdens of adulthood and go on a youthful adventure with my love: we would travel all around the world, we would go to rock concerts. Far out, groovy, wicked! I was in love and young enough to dare to do something that unusual and totally irresponsible.

*If I am not successful then at least I will have fun*, I thought. *Life is too short to spend it living from one day to another. I will take a break, a long break. We'll see what we'll do when we come back.*

But I was getting ahead of myself. I planned for a year maybe. Or half a year. As long as Ching Lan would want. Finally I was to be able to switch off, what I'd been longing to do all my life. A taste of pure youthfulness, independence, wildness and love. I could hardly wait to share all this with her.

## V. A SURPRISE

I GAVE THE DRIVER A CD AND ASKED HIM TO PLAY IT AS LOUD AS possible. Beforehand, I called the restaurant and asked Ching Lan's friend to send her out to get some vegetables exactly at four o'clock. I was holding a rose. Although Ching Lan had already tried to reach me by phone that day, I didn't pick up. I might have spoiled the surprise if I had answered the phone. At four o'clock I was waiting in front of the taxi from which China Girl was blaring at full volume. I really hoped she would like that.

A bit after four the door opened and she stepped out. She heard the music and looked to see what it was. When she saw me standing there her eyes lit up like they did a week ago when I told her about the surprise. With a look like this she could bring warmth to many a winter's day... She came running to me looking all aglow and threw herself on me. She hugged my waist with her legs and she felt as light as a feather. And she was mine! I held her in my arms and enjoyed the softness of her kisses.

"You came! You really came!" she kept repeating while she was kissing me. Like she wanted to say: there really is a God.

"I promised, didn't I?" I said with a smile.

"What about you? Have you kept your part of the bargain...?" I teased her while putting her on the ground again.

"And that is...?"

"Have you packed your bags?" I said and looked at her.

"Well, not really," she started to giggle. "But I can arrange everything.

Can you wait here, with me for a couple of days?"

"You mean I should sleep at your place instead of the hotel?"

"Yeah. I even have my own room," she said ironically and I felt that she had wanted to move for a very long time.

"How about you come stay with me at the hotel?"

"That's not a bad idea at all!" she said enthusiastically. She sounded sort of like a convict being set free after being sentenced to life. "And we can settle a couple of things about the journey. I have to tell you," her eyes were pretty moist at this point, "I didn't completely believe you would come back. That you would ever come back…"

"I'm here now and that's all that matters," I added softly. I felt I wanted to spend my life by her side no matter what. Especially because she seemed so full of life and at the same time so… fragile in my arms.

"Let me just tell them you came and then we can be off," she said playfully.

"Actually, I think everybody already knows," I said smiling. "They were a part of my plan. We can just go!"

"What? Also…"

"Yes. She actually doesn't need any vegetables. It was just an excuse to get you out and into my arms. Look," I said pointing at the window of their restaurant. There were about five girls looking out of the window and an older man who I thought must have been Ching Lan's father. Everybody waved at us joyfully.

"Admittedly, they are privy only to the first part of the story – that I came to visit you. As a surprise. But they don't know yet that you are leaving for… half a year. A year. As long as you want."

Ching Lan smiled. "For all my life," she whispered in my ear while gently biting on my earlobe. I felt electricity run through my entire body and I held her even closer to me.

## VI. TROUBLES

"**D**O YOU EVEN KNOW WHAT YOU ARE DOING?" said her younger sister Chang-juan.

"Of course I do," Ching Lan said with a voice that betrayed she was really in love. "I'm letting you have the restaurant and I'm leaving with him. We love each other. And that's that. I'm leaving."

While she was talking to her sister at the door I waited for her at the taxi feeling a bit anxious because we were already running late for our flight.

"Don't be a fool, Ching Lan. How can you just run off with a total stranger? You have a family here and safety..." her father added.

"But I don't have him," she said and gestured towards me. "I'll find a job..."

"Like you did in New York five years ago, you mean?" her other younger sister Dao-ming said sarcastically. "You know he isn't going to stay with you. No one has so far."

Ching Lan started walking. "You don't understand. Goodbye."

She started walking towards me but her steps seemed heavy and her eyes were moist and I could feel we wouldn't get very far. Her family was very important to her and they held her back and that would continue no matter where we would go. I walked towards her and stopped her. I held her hand and led her back to the restaurant. I had a feeling that they had purposely argued in English for my benefit. I got the hint and got involved.

"Chang-juan, Dao-ming, sir..." I started respectfully. It suddenly came to me that I had become quite an expert for Chinese names. Each name seemed so unique and special that it started to represent a challenge.

Especially because each name also had a meaning – Graceful Moon, Shining Path, Gorgeous Orchid...

"I really love Ching Lan and I will never allow for something to happen to her. I respect your concern that shows how much you love her. Even though she will live with me, we will visit you regularly. Traveling great distances, as you know, is not a problem anymore. There are different means of transport that have made the distances smaller than they used to be. I would like to ask you, though, for your... blessing. If you don't want her to go and be happy with me, then we won't go."

Ching Lan looked at me and I saw a mixture of astonishment and disappointment in her eyes but I knew I was doing the right thing. There was no way her family would choose to deny her happiness. Not in this way. In this way we would get peace, trust and permission, and that is worth much more than eloping.

Suddenly everyone was quiet. I didn't think I would surprise them that much. Now that the responsibility for Ching Lan's happiness fell on their shoulders they lost some of their earlier courage. Suddenly the villain disappeared and they had no one to blame and be angry at anymore...

Chang-juan was the first to speak. "I apologize for being angry... But you know, I only want what's best for you... I mean, if you are happy with him and if you will really visit us... Well, then..." She looked towards her father one more time feeling unsure but he didn't reveal his feelings in the least. "Then I have nothing against you going."

"I think so too," nodded Dao-ming. "And make sure you call us. I mean, call us frequently!" she said smiling.

"Ahem, ahem," her father cleared his throat coughing. "It won't go that easily."

We looked in the direction of the serious gentleman, who was wearing a brown cap with a short brim that went with his jacket. Life had left quite a few marks in the form of wrinkles on his face. "What about my permission, my blessing?"

Ching Lan gave him a puppy look.

"Come here, baby!" he said and spread his arms for a hug and smiled. "If he doesn't bring you back in one piece, I will show him all the illegal kung fu kicks and punches," he concluded. Then he turned to me, "You're really something, convincing my daughter like this in one week to follow you like little ducklings follow their mother. I hope she knows what she's doing," he added with a smile and shook my hand.

"If she doesn't know yet, I will convince her," I replied while giving his hand a firm shake.

When we were leaving the whole restaurant waved goodbye to us. Ching Lan sat very close to me on the narrow back seat of the taxi and I could feel how relieved she felt.

"You needn't have done that," she said caringly.

"But I made it better, didn't I?" I said stroking her cheek.

She looked at me and her eyes sparkled. She just said "Yes" and squeezed even closer to me.

## VII. LONDON

"I CAN HARDLY WAIT TO TAKE YOU TO MY PLACE..." I SAID TO HER, when we took our bags at the airport.

"... to unpack, right?" she asked inquisitively.

"Yes, that too," I agreed, when we arrived to the taxi.

"I must tell you that Chinese women are very traditional when it comes to intimacy. If you have something like that in mind, I'm afraid you'll have to wait till we are married..."

"No problem. I'll just marry you then," I said and smiled. I turned to the driver and shouted, "To St. Paul's, please."

He looked at me utterly confused and Ching Lan smiled.

"I'm sorry, I was just joking," I said quickly when Ching Lan started pulling on my sleeve.

"I can't believe you just did something like that."

"That's because I'm besotted by you."

"It's interesting how much love and madness we have in common," she commented.

Soon we came to my flat. Rose petals greeted us on the stairs. Obviously John, my neighbor, had kept his promise. I told him when to sprinkle the staircase with rose petals and he did it. And I gave him 20 quid to do it with positive thoughts. I loved spending money for Ching Lan. On the door, there were the words, 'Welcome home, Ching Lan'.

When she reached those words she took them off and held them to her heart. Her eyes filled up again.

"Now you are no longer gorgeous orchid, you are misty orchid," I joked when I came to her.

I hugged her, picked her up and carried her upstairs to the first floor. When we came to the door, I had some problems finding the key in my pocket while she was smiling and resting in my arms. When I finally managed to unlock the door, I carried her over the threshold like newlyweds usually do. I gave her a tour of the flat carrying her around in my arms:

"This is the kitchen, living room, bathroom and over there – it's the bedroom!" I said putting her down on the bed.

We started kissing and I took off her coat and scarf. She was so wonderful that I wanted to give her all the best things in this world. I wanted to be successful so I could give her all the money in this world. I wanted to be strong so I could be the best foundation for our family... I wanted to be gentle so I wouldn't hurt her. And I wanted to love her like no man had ever loved her before...

As I lay there supporting myself on my elbows, gazing down on her divine face, her beautiful dark eyes looked directly at me.

"You know... about the wedding, I didn't really mean that," she sighed while she wriggled lovingly in my arms.

"But I did," I said smiling and kissed her. "How would you like to get married? In Vegas, in a church, are you part of any religion I should join...?" I kept saying like I was reading a restaurant menu.

"Nothing special," she laughed at my joke. "The local registry office should do just fine."

Hearing her words I felt totally at peace. Like I wanted to hear them all my life.

"And the guests?" I went on. "I have 300 relatives. Most of them live in Africa."

"And those are...?"

"My dad and the rest of the 299 animals he takes pictures of."

"How about your mother?" she asked cautiously.

Then I continued more seriously.

"She's no longer with us. My dad and her were pretty close, though, but she... died ten years ago in a car crash."

She stroked my face. "I'm really sorry," she said and added, "I also don't have a mother."

"On a more pleasant note," I said not wanting my love to feel sad on the very first day of our new life. "This is a schedule you can change around all you want," I said pulling a list of concerts I had compiled from under the bed. I felt pretty proud of myself having succeeded to compile a list of good performers as well as locations that perfectly complemented each other. We would start in London, visit New York, San Francisco, Los Angeles and a part of Africa where I wanted to introduce her to my dad, and finally come back to London. Like our own private little tour.

"I love it," she was amazed when she saw my plan. She started to kiss me again when we heard discreet coughing behind us. We turned around and there was John, my neighbor.

"I'm sorry to just walk in on you like that. It was open I thought maybe I could help somehow," he said.

"No big deal, John," I said and introduced my new girlfriend.

## VIII. LONDON AND NEW YORK

"**Y**OU'VE REALLY CHOSEN VERY GOOD ARTISTS," ADDED CHING LAN when she went through my list for the second time in the morning. "I'm glad you approve," I said enthusiastically with my mouth full. Having breakfast with her seemed divine. Having her share the table with me felt fantastic.

"I wanted to choose artists who played rock music with occasional digressions into pop, and the music had to be romantic," I explained. I didn't want to take her to concerts that were too loud and wild. I chose the following artists: Bryan Adams, Robbie Williams, Jon Bon Jovi, Sting and Jesse Roy.

"We can start tomorrow," she said when she noticed the date of the first concert.

"Sure."

"And we can finish in six months' time," she concluded when she went over the dates. "You have to stop when it's the most..."

"The most interesting, right. OK. Deal."

So we started with preparations. We packed our bags and prepared our documents. I took her around London to see all the sights before we left. We didn't hire any guides, of course; I was responsible for our itinerary. And because there were many things I didn't know, I spiced up my tour with some facts that weren't exactly true. For example:

"This is Big Ben. It was named after the architect that designed it. He had a very big... nose," I added meaningfully. Ching Lan laughed. After three days of sightseeing we flew to New York. When we landed in New York, I remembered my youth and was overflowing with positive memories. Ching Lan was by my side and this was the first time it occurred to me that remembering the times when I wanted to succeed was not so bad after all. I was alive and I had a dream. I could still make it, it wasn't too late. *I still want to be successful*, I realized. *But this time for her, not for myself.*

After unpacking at the Park Central Hotel, Ching Lan said she wished to go for a walk. We went out and walked past our high school.

We were greeted by the castle-like building front. This time it looked even more fairytale-like. It felt like walking past our own castle. The grayness of the building reminded me of times gone by that painted the shadows of sadness and loss. And at the same time the colorful main entrance seemed to foretell our bright future…

I stopped in front of the door. I wanted to surprise her.

"I know it's too late but… can you imagine that this is happening five years ago?"

She looked a bit bewildered not knowing what I had in mind.

"Well, it goes like this: we've just finished school. We come out. You wish to wave goodbye to me and I stop you," I held her by the hand, "and speak to you."

"Ching Lan," I said.

"Yes?" she replied quickly assuming the role of herself five years ago.

"I really like you… Do you think we could… Is there a chance you could be my girlfriend?" I said reluctantly like a high school boy. She smiled.

"Well, you know, I'll have to think about that."

"What?!" I asked incredulously. "The script says, YES! Now, immediately!"

She granted me my wish. "Yes, yes, immediately, yes, of course." We kissed and hugged.

"Oh, I almost forgot. Would you like to go to a Bryan Adams concert with me?"

"Yes, immediately, yes," she kept repeating.

We spent the whole afternoon caressing each other and walking in the park which seemed to start feeling warmer in the February day. In the evening we surrendered to the romantic nature of the concert…

## IX. SAN FRANCISCO

WE ATTENDED THE NEXT TWO CONCERTS IN SAN FRANCISCO. We had two entire months to change the location, do the sightseeing and start a life there. The city seemed less hectic and much cleaner than New York and the air was also less polluted. We hadn't planned hiring any guides so I decided to improvise here too. And later we also bought some guidebooks to learn about the city. But we had a lot of fun guessing who had left an enormous bow and arrow that was stuck in the ground in the park. We saw a big golden heart on some stairs and Ching Lan posed with the heart like she was giving it to me…

One day I took her to Chinatown.

"This is a very old and traditional Chinatown…" I started imitating a tourist guide.

"You know what? It really bothers me that there is a Chinatown whenever I go," she said almost angry. "Wherever I go, I feel like I hadn't left home at all. But I would like to see the world, I would like to be a tourist! But I can't be because wherever I go, I always end up back home!"

This time it was her that made me laugh. She was right in a way. We gave Chinatown a wide berth and started to discover the beauties of the rest of San Francisco.

Many times we just stood and looked at the numerous beaches, people or the mist rising above the ocean. It was truly beautiful. The Golden Gate Bridge greeted the San Franciscans dreamily every morning and the city seemed to us more than romantic with it cleanliness, beauty and a quiet dreamy charm.

The first concert we went to was Robbie Williams. We had a great time singing, dancing and kissing while listening to his romantic songs. She smiled all the time and I was ecstatic to be here. Both of us wore jeans and T-shirts feeling young enough to be irresponsible and crazy enough to go on an adventure like this.

I could feel that Ching Lan was opening up to me more and more. I felt there was no way back. I also confided in her and told her some details and dark secrets from my life I hadn't shared with anybody before. Some people might have thought them small and irrelevant, but Ching Lan managed to accept and comprehend all the subtleties of the stories I shared with her. Nobody had ever listened to me with so much interest and love. I had the feeling she really was the one I wanted to spend the rest of my life with. Even though we had only been together for a couple of months. When you know, you just know.

During an especially cold night, when the nature additionally encouraged us to hold our bodies against each other, we were keeping warm under a warm blanket. It was more than apparent that both of us were really turned on. Ching Lan tried to encourage me with kisses but I really wanted to wait.

"We can get married right after our tour," she almost begged me.

"I know but…"

"What do you mean but? Don't you fancy me?" she turned away trying to show me how offended she was. I felt then what power women had over us.

"I do. That's the reason I want to wait."

"Well, please yourself," she said and rolled to the other end of the bed. I could hear the pitter-patter of raindrops against the window and I really wanted to hang out with her.

"Ching Lan…"

"Good night!" she said feeling offended. I didn't want her to take this so seriously. I just thought she was way to precious to… But I was also having problems resisting her intoxicating beauty. Instead of trying to persuade her with words, I decided to act.

I slowly caressed her shoulder and I felt her body shiver. When I reached the buttons I stared to unbutton her pajamas slowly. When she turned to face me I surrendered to my burning desire, to continue what I was doing and she started to undress me too. I had given up trying to undo the buttons one by one and just pulled the fabric with one quick jerk. The buttons went flying and she gave a shriek of repressed passion.

"Finally," she said and then we spoke no more. The whole night we spent in joyful merging with each other. Her hand led me where she wanted to be touched and I was in heaven while she teased me with her gentle caresses…

I woke into a cold morning but felt great happiness feeling her breath on my shoulder. I enjoyed her presence for a while and then tiptoed out of bed and to the telephone and ordered room service. I kept the door open so they wouldn't wake Ching Lan. I quickly gave the man a tip and went back inside.

I put the tray in front of her and stroked her cheek.

"Good morning, Mrs. Ching Lan Blake," I said as she was slowly opening her big eyes.

"What? Wow, is this for me?" she still tried to make sense of everything.

"For you and I guess a little bit for me too," I added.

"Considering what happened yesterday, we are obviously married," I said while I bit into a slice of fresh toast with a divine fish pate, "if not according to the law at least symbolically."

She smiled and added with her mouth full: "Oh, that's why you called me Ching Lan Blake," she paused and continued, "well, it doesn't sound that bad."

# X. LOS ANGELES

Sᴀɴ Fʀᴀɴᴄɪsᴄᴏ ʀᴇᴘʀᴇsᴇɴᴛᴇᴅ ᴀ ᴍᴀᴊᴏʀ ᴍɪʟᴇsᴛᴏɴᴇ ɪɴ ᴏᴜʀ ʀᴇʟᴀᴛɪᴏɴsʜɪᴘ so we found it pretty hard to leave. There was something special about it... Some kind of inner beauty. Like Ching Lan possessed. I used to think that 'all Chinese women looked the same'. But now I would recognize the eyes of my love in a sea of other Chinese eyes. Her face was more heart-shaped and more open than the others. Her full lips were a rarity among Chinese women. And her pure soul shined like a diamond through her beautiful dark eyes.

We felt the city's vibration immediately as we landed at the airport. It was much more open and less mysterious. In the following three months we were going to attend these concerts: Jon Bon Jovi, Sting and Jesse Roy. I chose the first one, she chose Sting and the third one was a must because both of us knew the artist. I only knew him for a year but still... The leaflet said: 'An unforgettable experience and fantastic stage effects. A must-see!'

We soon got used to the city that never slept. We enjoyed strolling along the colorful Walk of Fame. I suddenly realized that I knew quite a lot of people – be it schoolmates, friends, relatives – who had been blessed with real success and fame. Maybe that was the reason I was craving it so much myself. When Ching Lan noticed my absent-mindedness, she asked me if everything was all right. I told her what I was thinking about.

"I think you should consider yourself lucky," she said smiling. I had a feeling that she couldn't care less about success or fame. "You know so many successful people to be able to learn from them. Not envy them."

"It's not that I envy th…"

Ching Lan interrupted me by pointing a finger at me. "Excuse me? You should listen to your voice – do you envy them or not?" she went on smiling. She could read me like an open book, of course.

"Well, you're right. I do envy them. But that's pretty normal, isn't it?"

"My father used to say: envy signifies the following thought: if he/she were not here, I would be in his/her place. Do you realize how poisonous this emotion is? The worst acts spring from this emotion. In a way you want to neutralize the person who supposedly stands in your way."

I marveled at the wisdom of the old man but at the same time was not willing to accept it yet.

"So you're dating a murderer."

"Not yet," she smiled when she noticed my long face. "Now that you know this, you can start thinking differently and feel positive emotions about these people."

"I don't have to feel gracious about their success," I said holding her even closer to me, "because I'm much better off than they are. They can be envious about my gorgeous orchid!" I said joking. And so we came to the end of the Walk of Fame and I felt a bit better.

I really enjoyed seeing palm trees everywhere around me. The atmosphere was relaxed and open. We came across Chinatown again and Ching Lan seemed a bit desperate. I took a picture of her posing like she couldn't believe how it was possible that she had arrived home again.

*I will make a great album with these photos*, I thought.

In the next three months we saw many sights and we also sought out places where we could be alone. The time was running way too fast. Bon Jovi's performance was very youthful despite his age, and Sting charmed us with his romantic music. But when it came to Jesse Roy concert, well that was a bit… different.

## XI. A FATEFUL TURN OF EVENTS

"**W**HAT? A hundred dollars for a ticket? Are you out of your mind?" I raged at the ticket office.

"Relax, Derek. It's just a ticket," Ching Lan tried to make me calm down.

"This guy is quite insane! One hundred dollars – do they throw in a washing machine or what?" I couldn't calm down.

"Maybe the show is really worth it. My friend…"

"No way! Let's go," I said and pulled out of the line. She stopped me and looked at me seriously.

"I had no idea you were so mean. You don't want to pay 200 dollars and that's only because you know Jesse. You don't think it's possible his concert could be worth that much money. But inside you feel that if he wasn't there, you might be in his place."

"That's simply not true. I'm not even a musician."

"It doesn't matter. The feelings of envy are the same. When you can think straight, please let me know," she said and turned away.

*I might have really overreacted a bit*, I thought.

"I'm sorry, Ching Lan, I just…" I wanted to make up a plausible excuse for my behavior but I couldn't find one. When she looked me in the eye, I realized one more time that any pretending would have been pointless.

"I've been craving success all my life and… when I see what some people can afford… do you know how much money that is? Twenty thousand seats multiplied by 100 dollars…"

"And do you think feeling like this will change anything? This pain that you feel because you are not them, this anger that they have made it and you haven't, this terror how poor you are and how rich they are? Do you really think that having these thoughts will help you or us?"

"No," I mumbled.

"Congratulations! You've managed to destroy a perfectly romantic evening. I don't want to go to the concert anymore."

Now all of a sudden I was the one who really wanted us to go. I had a feeling that I had made a really rotten impression on her. Like I didn't have the two hundred dollars. Like I was the most incompetent person in this world… I desperately wanted to go. After she had already turned to walk away I walked up to her, nervously grabbed her by the shoulder and turned her to face me.

"But I want to go, Ching Lan," I said childishly.

"We are not going."

"Please yourself, but I'm still buying the tickets," I insisted. I went to the box office and stood in the line again. While I was waiting I kept looking towards Ching Lan who had moved off to a more solitary place. I could see that she was still looking away. We argued for so long that dusk had already set in. I noticed a blue and light-green neon inscription that invited the visitors to buy the tickets. The smooth sidewalk glittered in the clear evening and a saw that a pretty long line had formed behind me. I desperately wanted to go after her but I had decided not to go anywhere without the tickets.

When it was finally my turn, I said almost victoriously:

"Two tickets for Jesse Roy, please."

The cashier looked at me a bit surprised not knowing what my tone meant. Because I was so busy buying the tickets I didn't notice that a fight between two gangs had broken out on the other side of the street. I guessed somebody owed somebody something.

When I put my tickets away I noticed that a guy was threatening someone with a gun. The guy who was being threatened quickly grabbed his aggressor by the hand and moved it away from his face. A shot went off. The police arrived and arrested both guys. Ching Lan, who was watching from the other side of the road, suddenly fell to the ground. I was there immediately.

"What's wrong?" I asked quickly.

"I have a pain in my chest…" she complained. I looked at her chest and noticed a dark red stain which was getting bigger and bigger on her left side.

"I can't believe this," I said more to myself, "you've been shot!"

I started shouting in panic. "Ambulance! Somebody call an ambulance. Police!"

"There's no need," she said quietly. "It just stings a bit." But the stain kept getting bigger. Her breathing became labored and I had no idea what to do. I desperately tried to remember what to do from my first aid course…

"Can anybody do CPR? She has a bullet in her chest," I kept screaming while a crowd gathered around us. The people were just standing and looking. Obviously nobody was able to do anything else but look. Although we were not alone I couldn't care less. I decided to keep her awake.

"Ching Lan, please forgive me for my behavior," I said to her.

She looked at me peacefully. "It's not a big deal."

"Well, I think it is. If I am envious, I am like… the weakest person in the world, like a murderer. I understand that now. I know. I want to be strong, for you."

"You are strong. Just being able to talk about it proves that. Because you don't defend yourself," she said and smiled, as her face was growing paler by the second. The pool of blood on her chest seemed to deepen visibly. I remembered that in the practical part of my first aid exam for my driver's license, we had to bandage something. In case of hemorrhaging from the chest, we were taught to bandage tightly the veins that led to the heart. I took off my shirt and fixed it firmly around her left arm. I really wanted to help her.

"I bought the tickets, you know," I said to her when I was done.

"Oh, that really wasn't necessary," she replied.

"Actually, it was. This is a first-class show, just for us," I went on romantically.

"For me just being with you feels first-class," she smiled. Then she closed her eyes.

"Ching Lan, please try to stay awake. I've called an ambulance," I said quickly.

Her breathing was shallow and almost inaudible. "But... I... have to."

I held her by the hand that lay limp beside her. I began to panic even more.

*This can't be happening. Everything will be OK. This can't be happening,* my head buzzed.

The ambulance arrived and I started shouting feeling helpless: "Over here, over here, come quickly!"

They came running and put her on a gurney. They pushed her to the ambulance and I followed them.

"Are you family?"

"Yes, I'm her boyfriend," I regretted not being able to say I was her fiancé or husband...

We rushed to the nearest hospital. The buildings had an icy shine in the darkness of the night. Although the night was warm I shivered all over. Two paramedics that had already started the CPR worked faster and faster. One of them gave the instructions to the driver.

"Faster! Turn on the siren! We must hurry!"

When we reached the emergency they took her in and I ran after them.

Soon we arrived at the intensive care unit. Of course I wanted to go in.

"Wait outside, please!" the doctor ordered me pushing me aside. If he had known how much she meant to me, if he had felt what I felt, he would have understood me. The only thing I could do was stand in front of the door feeling totally powerless and repeating to myself, *I'm sure everything will be all right, it must be, God, please, definitely, it must be...*

I waited for two long hours. I didn't go anywhere. I sweated and repeated my mantra in front of the door. Tears kept running down my cheeks and I had never before felt so anxious. I had a mind-splitting headache and I was sitting on the floor because the nearest bench seemed too far away. I heard some noises and beeping but I had no idea what they meant. That must have been two of the longest hours in my life.

When the doctor came from the room, I got up. He was surprised finding me so close-by.

"How is she? Can I see her? Have you managed to remove the bullet?" questions started pouring out of me. I was convinced that they were successful, having been in the operating room for so long. Ching Lan was going to stay for a couple of hours and then we would go back to the hotel. And in a couple of days we would go to the concert and all this nonsense about the tickets would be long forgotten…

The doctor looked down.

"Actually, I think you should sit down," he said and put his hand on my shoulder. I pushed it off.

"I'm quite all right, thank you." He really started to annoy me.

"Your… friend… I'm afraid we couldn't save her."

When you watch a movie and somebody is given such devastating news, you usually witness great acting from the side of the actors who start crying, waving their arms and behaving strangely in all sorts of ways. But I had already cried enough. I just wanted to see my love and that was that. I didn't believe what the man in the white coat was telling me. Ching Lan was conscious not so long ago. And I was going to see her one way or another.

"OK then, smart ass," I said, "where's the camera? I know she is alive. Can I see her, please?"

"You didn't understand me correctly," he said trying to sound understanding. But I interrupted him.

"She's here, right?" I said pointing to the door. I went in.

Ching Lan was lying on the bed with her arms by her side. She looked like she was sleeping.

"I knew you were just asleep," I said quietly. She still looked pale but I hoped that her cheeks would become red again when she had got some sleep. The hospital staff surrounding me looked eerily somber. I got to the bed. She was totally still. Her full and now pale lips were completely closed and they seemed to rest. When I looked at them closely I saw that they were completely still too. Her nose was also totally still. If she had been asleep, she would have been breathing. I touched the vein on her neck, but nothing moved. Like touching a small dead tube.

But she was still warm. They managed to disguise her smell that had brought me so much happiness in the past couple of months with disinfectants and other substances… I realized Ching Lan was really dead. I stretched out my hand and stroked her hair… No response. I yearned for her to open her big loving dark eyes again and like so many times before bring light to the room… To hear her say, "I'm just teasing you," and see her get up. But no. Her body was lying on the bed like a beautiful but cold mannequin. I couldn't believe my eyes.

"Ching Lan…" I managed to say before tears rushed down my cheeks again. I held her close to me. I just held her for some time. Soon I had a feeling she twitched a little.

"She's moved, she's still alive!" I shouted. I looked around the room and saw there were only some junior members of staff left. "Please try again," I begged.

"What you've felt are reflexes after electroshocks," one of them explained to me.

"I don't care," I barked. "She must be alive!" I grabbed hold of two paddle electrodes and thought about where to switch the defibrillator on. They had already called the doctor and the security.

"Sir, please come with us," a security guard said with a serious voice. But I didn't let him disturb me. What if she was still alive?

"I will not just stand there if nobody wants to help me," I insisted. Suddenly I felt a firm grip and I was being dragged away from the bed. I resisted, pushed him off and continued where I had stopped.

"He is stronger than I thought," said a fat black security guard and grabbed me again. This time his push was so strong that I quickly ended up on the other side of the room where other guards had been waiting for me. They dragged me out of the room kicking and screaming. I felt a gentle sting on my backside and I realized I must have been injected with something. I didn't remember how I ended up in a hospital bed.

## XII. ANOTHER SURPRISE

WHEN I OPENED MY EYES I SAW A BLINKING HOSPITAL LIGHT IN front of me. My head hurt and my mouth was dry. I decided to move to my side. When I wanted to move using my hands I realized I was tied to my bed. I started wriggling but couldn't get loose. I heard some voices.

"He's awake," said a woman's voice at the door.

"Is he swearing again?" asked a man's voice.

"No, now he is just shaking his arms," was the answer.

*You would be shaking them too if you were tied to the bed*, I thought. Then the door opened.

"How are we feeling today, Mr. Blake?" a doctor addressed me kindly. But the tone of his voice was a little peculiar. He didn't seem to take me as an ordinary patient. I had a feeling that he wouldn't take me seriously no matter what I said to him.

"Where am I?" I asked with a husky voice.

"Well, we have already covered that, haven't we?" he replied kindly.

"I'm serious. Please tell me," I went on. The last thing that I remembered was some kind of pushing in a hospital corridor… Gradually it all started coming back to me…

*A hospital room… A body lying on the bed… Ching Lan, my love… is dead. I have to see her! What's happened? Where the hell am I?*

I twitched and grabbed the bondages on the bed wanting to tear them out.

"Where am I? Where is Ching Lan? What's going on?"

"Oh, not that again. Nurse, come please," called the doctor.

A nurse appeared and started preparing an injection. When I realized it was so serious I tried to calm down a bit. I really wanted to find out where I was and how I could get out.

"I apologize for my behavior," I said. "Could you please just tell me where I am and where my fiancée Ching Lan is?" I called her my fiancée deliberately to make it sound a bit more serious.

"Your fiancée?" the doctor repeated after me and looked at me sideways. "The file stated 'girlfriend'."

"We had a secret engagement," I lied. "We were going to announce it in a week or so."

"Well, you know what happened to her, don't you?" the doctor asked me seriously. Of course I remembered what had happened. I made a grimace and tried to calm down again so that I wouldn't get the early goodnight wish in the form of the cocktail the nurse had already prepared for me in the syringe.

"Yes… I know." I sighed. "You must let me go. I must inform her family. The funeral…"

The doctor and the nurse exchanged meaningful looks. "There has already been a funeral. Ages ago. Since you were in that state, we contacted her relatives who flew over from Tianjin and organized everything…"

"Is that so? When was that?" I started to feel angry again.

"Well, about two months ago…"

Two months? I've been here for two months. And I've missed the funeral! And these people think I'm crazy? My God! How could this be?

"What? The funeral was two months ago?" I asked angrily. No wonder I had to be injected with something every time I woke up. No wonder I forgot everything every time I woke up. It was way too horrible for me to handle!

"What a shame! I was so pleased with the progress he seemed to be making. Nurse," he gestured towards me while I was struggling and shaking all over. Maybe this time she wouldn't be able to stick the needle into me.

The doctor walked up and routinely touched my thigh. The nurse stuck a needle into my skin and injected the contents, and then moved away.

"You should know we only want what's best for you," the doctor said. Soon I was engulfed by darkness.

## XIII. ILLUSIONS

"*A*RE YOU ALL RIGHT?" *I heard a familiar voice ask. A pair of dark eyes filled with love was looking at me.*

"*What kind of question is that?" I was surprised to see her again. "You better tell me if you are all right?" I replied. "I only recently found out that you're…"*

"*That I'm what? Here?" she said and pointed around herself. The bright green grass full of colorful flowers stood out from the rest of the surroundings. I was laying in the green softness, marveling at the round-shaped architecture around me. Quite a few domes were glittering around us and it seemed that they were some sort of buildings.*

"*Do you like it here?" she asked pointing around.*

"*Very much," I replied. It seemed that both of us still knew we belonged together, even if this time everything was coming along entirely differently… We heard a call and turned around. Only then I noticed that I was lying on a bluish-green platform. A blond-haired woman came up to us.*

"*Derek, are you OK?" she asked me.*

'*Why does everybody keep asking me that? Yes, I'm quite fine, thank you,' I thought.*

*My love was still holding me in her arms, stroking my hair. "Congratulations, Derek," she said and kissed me…*

*I felt the wind blow all over my body and noticed my pants were torn. What on earth happened to me? I closed my eyes and surrendered to the wind, hoping it would clear up my memory…*

When I opened my eyes again I was in the hospital room. I had been dreaming again. It was the first time in quite a while that people considered me normal… After three months in a nuthouse you start asking yourself all sorts of questions… Who was I? Why was I here? Would I ever be able to get out of this place? What really happened? I asked to make a telephone call but my wish was denied.

I decided not to put up a fight anymore. I knew it was always followed by a shot, but this time I really didn't want that anymore. I had a feeling something stirred in the room. I raised my head to see better. I saw a human silhouette in the dim light of the room. When he saw that I noticed him, he came closer. It was a young man with brown hair. Although I didn't know him, he seemed familiar when he came closer to my bed.

"Hello, Derek," he greeted me quietly.

"Do we know each other?"

"Yes, we do. But we haven't seen each other for quite some time. My name is Aaron."

I couldn't remember where I knew him from. I decided to be honest about it. It was obvious that this man was taking me much more seriously than the others and he didn't seem to think I was bonkers at all.

"I'm really sorry but I don't remember where I know you from…" I said wanting to hear some details.

"Well, that's not even that important. If I started explaining now, you wouldn't believe me anyway," he smiled revealing slightly askew but still symmetrical teeth.

"Our main task now is to get you away from here. Please do exactly as I tell you, OK?"

I agreed not having much to lose anyway.

"I'm going to visit you during the day today. Please don't say anything, no matter what I say. Whatever they ask you, whatever they want you to tell them, doesn't matter. Your only task is to be quiet. OK?"

"OK. How long should I be quiet?"

"Until we are out. Promise? Otherwise I can't help you."

"OK. I promise."

"Thank you. And now you should get some sleep. We have a difficult day ahead of us."

I closed my eyes. Then I wanted to ask him something, so I opened them again.

"Hey, Aaron?"

I looked around the room and saw it was empty. Now I started to believe I was really off my rocker. Feeling completely desperate I leaned my head against the pillow that felt a bit sweaty. In the combination of hope that I might not have imagined all that and terror that my hallucinations could be so vivid I tried to go to sleep. After struggling for a couple of hours I was finally blessed.

## XIV. THE GAME

I WAS AWAKENED BY A SOUND OF KEYS. I heard voices coming from the outside. The doctor was talking to the nurse and another person. I decided not to speak no matter what happened. I really didn't want any shots anymore. So I wasn't going to cooperate. I just wanted to know what was going on... but obviously that wasn't possible. Not in this way.

"This way, Mr. Blake..." said the doctor.

My ears pricked up. *Mr. Blake? I'm Mr. Blake!* I felt like I was in a horror movie where the main protagonist was going bonkers and having extremely vivid hallucinations all at the same time.

*Great! And now I'll meet myself,* I thought. Like the whole thing wasn't surreal enough! As a matter of fact, that was the only strange thing that still hadn't happened to me!

First the doctor and the nurse came into the room and behind them the brown-haired man. I recognized him immediately.

"I hope I'm not too late," said Aaron and touched my head. "Derek, can you hear me?"

I stayed quiet, like we had agreed.

"Oh, no! We'd better hurry," said Aaron sounding very important. The doctor, who was less and less sure what was going on, asked quickly, "What do you mean 'hurry'? The patient is receiving professional medical care..."

"That's exactly why. Don't get me wrong, doctor, but this disease runs in the family. Our father got it too. After our mom died. It started with hysteria and then he became dumb. He was like that for a couple of weeks before he died."

The doctor started to draw logical connections and he must have remembered my outbursts because he nodded his head.

"What can we do for him?" he inquired. I was glad Aaron was able to make such an impression.

"It's an absolute must that he comes home immediately where he'll be able to see the greenery and our family forest." I almost couldn't help but laugh hearing him going on like that. It sounded like some pathetic attempt at poetry.

"Well, if you really think that will help him, I cannot say no. But it is advisable that he comes for a check-up and some tests…"

"How in God's name can you suggest that? You can see that in these conditions the disease is progressing faster and faster! This is a mental disease and being in this institution is only making it worse for the patient. I know this doesn't seem to make sense but we could say the same thing about human psyche, couldn't we? He only got worse here!" he concluded convincingly.

"Well, if you really think so…"

"I know so. I saw what it did to my father…"

"OK then. I'll prepare all the documents for his discharge," the doctor agreed. I was amazed how easy it was.

"And please hurry," Aaron went on. "Every minute counts."

The doctor left the room and the nurse followed him. Aaron looked at me and smiled. I was really grateful and I guess he noticed it.

"It's not over yet," he told me. "Please be quiet until we are really outside."

The doctor returned quickly and gave us the discharge papers. After what seemed like an eternity, they took off my bondages and I noticed that my wrists were totally bruised. I was really happy to be free again and at the same time I wanted to strangle the person who had got me here in the first place. I hadn't done it myself. It didn't seem plausible that I would have been put in this place just because I had a mild panic attack at the death of my love. I'm sure it is hard for people to deal with news like that. And instead of just expressing their condolences they put me in a nuthouse... I would find out what had really happened. I was free at last!

I was put in a wheelchair. I realized how my body appreciated a different position from lying. I was looking forward to every second I would be able to spend in freedom.

"Goodbye then, Mr. Blake," said the doctor and shook Aaron's hand. He must have introduced himself as my brother or something.

"Thank you for everything. Take care!" Aaron replied.

He pushed me along endless corridors and many times we came to check points where we had to show my discharge papers. I felt like getting up and breaking into a run. But this would only lead me back to where I never wanted to go again... So I tried to calm down as much as possible and wait for us to get out of that place. When we came out, the air was totally different than inside. Now that I felt its freshness enter my lungs I didn't think it unusual anymore that people went even crazier inside. One reason was purely biological – a lack of quality oxygen.

We went down an access alley where a taxi was waiting for us.

"Will you tell me who you are and where I know you from now?"

"There'll be plenty of time for that," he replied quickly. "To the airport, please," he ordered the driver.

"Where are we going?"

"It's time for you to leave this city. Put this on, I think it's your size," he said handing me a pair of jeans and a T-shirt. The sun had just come out from behind the clouds and I realized it was pretty warm.

"What did you expect in the middle of July?" smiled Aaron.

"July?" I said surprised.

"Well, we have a lot of catching up to do," he said looking in the distance.

I changed, looking forward to finding out all the answers.

## XV. THE TRUTH REVEALED

AT THE AIRPORT WE WAITED IN THE LINE FOR NEW YORK.
"Oh, this is where we're going," I said wanting to make conversation. During the taxi ride our roles seemed to change – I was talking and asking questions and he was getting more and more quiet.

The flight seemed to take ages since Aaron still refused to speak. About half an hour before landing I said to him:

"I don't understand why you refuse to speak since you decided to rescue me."

"Because I don't want to answer your questions just yet."

"May I ask why not?"

"Because I don't want you to make a scene," he concluded. Like I was a child. As a matter of fact, he looked much younger than me.

When we finally arrived I was greeted by memories. I remembered every spot where Ching Lan and I went and the airport also seemed to be, in a way... ours. I felt a sharp pain in my chest and I realized that maybe the time has come for me to start grieving like a normal person. Without being tied to the bed...

Aaron smiled.

"Maybe now it is a good time to tell you who had you committed," he said loudly. The people around us greeted each other loudly and we could have screamed our vocal cords out and no one would have heard us.

"Who?" I asked quickly.

"Me," he said calmly.

"What?!" I shouted back. I was glad I was able to shout as much as I wanted. But I knew that I wouldn't have minced my words with him even if we had been alone. Even if he had chosen to share this with me in the middle of a classical concert. And he knew that.

"Can you even begin to realize what you did to me?!" I started. "I was asking myself for months if there was something wrong with me and what had really happened! They didn't even let me make a phone call! Do you know how it feels to be tied to the bed for so long? I wouldn't wish that on my mortal enemy – but I guess you didn't think twice about doing this to me! You should be chained somewhere!" Then I added some not too pleasant names, whatever came to my mind.

"Just let me know when you're done," he said calmly looking in front of himself. "But remember – what I did was for your own good. I have my limits too. I could easily turn you over to the police…"

I realized he was serious and said no more. He was stronger than he appeared. He made decisions for me like he was my owner. Like he bought himself a slave and now he got to decide what would happen to him. I found this extremely offensive, more than lying in a mental institution. But I swallowed my pride and decided to try to speak to the tyrant in a civilized manner. I would find out why he sent me there, what had happened and how to get rid of him. But until I got those answers I would have to be as… refined as possible.

## XVI. A WALK

THE TAXI DRIVER TOOK US TO A HOUSE WHERE WE LEFT OUT THINGS while he waited for us. After all those months, I wasn't even sure where my things and documents were and that didn't seem so important anymore. Like he was reading my thoughts, he said quickly:

"I guess you don't really care but your things and documents are in a suitcase in the house."

We quietly put our suitcases in the hall and sat in the taxi again. It took us to the Central Park.

"Oh, it's so much easier to breathe here, isn't it?" he said. I thought about my reply. And at the same time I tried to remember where I knew him from. If I knew more about him, it would be easier for me to make him tell me more about himself... I studied his moves, his face when he wasn't looking at me, his slightly askew teeth and his British accent, which he occasionally couldn't disguise... He was about seventeen years old. And he said that we hadn't seen each other for quite some time. What could that punk know about me?

"Yes, you're right," I said trying to sound friendly.

"So what did you want to ask me?" he suddenly became very helpful. But I was still studying him.

"Have you figured it out who I am?" he said and laughed playfully. But I didn't feel like playing games. At least not with a person who was that cruel.

"Well, not yet."

"No?" he looked at me surprised. "Well, I guess it's been a long time…"

*I've just about had it,* I thought. *This punk hasn't even been in this world for long. And now he is trying to sound smart like he was at least fifty years old.*

"I'm fifty-five years old, believe it or not," he replied calmly to my thought.

I smiled. He was testing me again how crazy I was.

"Insanity depends on the viewpoint. All the great men were considered insane in their time. I could easily be certified as insane. You've been doing it all the time."

I didn't know what to say to him. He took me by surprise. It was the first time after Ching Lan that somebody could read me like an open book. At the thought of Ching Lan I felt a sharp pain in my chest again.

"Well, if you really don't want to ask me, I'll tell you myself. I made sure you were put in that asylum for one reason only: because I didn't want you to feel sorry for yourself like you're doing now. Finding your mate was really a precious and beautiful experience but now she's gone. Even if you mourn her for all eternity, this will not bring her back. Your tears will bring nobody back from the dead."

When he was saying that I felt resentment rising up in me. This punk didn't know what he was talking about. He had absolutely no idea what it felt like to have one of your loved ones die.

"Grieving depends on the perspective, too. There is a tribe in Australia that mourns when a child is born – they believe it is very painful for a soul to become trapped in a small body. And they rejoice when a person dies – because they are finally free again. It all depends on the perspective. If you think what I'm saying doesn't make so much sense, you should know that I've experienced the bitterness of loss and grieving on my own skin. I had been wallowing in depression for twenty years until I was saved by my son and his girlfriend. If they hadn't been so strong, I wouldn't be here today."

He looked at me one more time and I got a brainwave. His eyes were blue… but they used to be a different color… His hair was brown… but it used to be white. His face, drooping cheeks that now looked so firm on

the young body... Principal Davies... Was that really possible?
"Anything is possible," he said calmly. "But you need to overcome a lot of your own darkness to realize that," he said with bitterness in his voice. "I almost died because of grieving. I went completely insane and I killed. Please, don't tell me this emotion is useful because it's not. It is one of the biggest hindrances that prevent us to act according to the laws of nature. Had I acted according to the laws of nature, I might even have made contact with her. But I had been drowning for seventeen years before my son opened my eyes."

I coughed and spoke for the first time without calculating anything. "And why exactly did you decide to have me committed?"

"Because I didn't want you to make the same mistake as I made. When you were there you thought about other things. You dreamt about good things. You focused away from sadness – you thought about Ching Lan only now and then. She was by your side all the time. Of course you were too busy to notice her. But you did dream about her."

I wanted to say something but he interrupted me.

"When I was informed that my wife was dead – and believe me I really loved her – I was free to do anything. Of course I was swallowed up by sadness. I was surrounded by all kinds of shadows and dark vibrations... thoughts. I bought a lot of equipment in the hope of making contact with her. My thoughts became more and more intensive until I had a feeling that I could hear them. I started paying attention and connected with them even more. They whispered all sorts of things to me. That Ina was harmful, that Ravi was looking to hurt me professionally, that if I hurt Ina, I would be able to make contact with my wife and so on. All this is madness. And immediately when you choose sadness you choose to participate in this madness. No matter how far you come. In a way, you were protected from that."

"From myself?"

"That's right."

I was still angry with him in a way. But everything that he told me seemed to make perfect sense. I couldn't defend myself no matter how much I thought I was right. While we were walking in the park, a young woman with curly blond hair came up to us.

## XVII. THE INTRODUCTION

"HELLO DEREK, I'M GLAD TO SEE YOU'RE FEELING BETTER," SHE greeted me smiling like we knew each other from Adam.

"Can somebody please explain to me what's going on? I really don't know her," I managed to utter.

"Oh, certainly," she stopped and almost curtsied. "My name is Keisha. You are right, we really haven't met yet," she confirmed. "But I've heard so much about you. From Jesse."

"Jesse Roy?" I asked surprised. So he did remember me!

"That's the one. You went to the same school, didn't you?"

"Well, it was just for a year but…"

"And you wrote the first lyrics for his songs…" Keisha reminded me.

"Well, I guess that's true."

"You see. Then you must be the right Derek!" she concluded. She radiated happiness and gracefulness. Keisha looked back and I saw a group of people approaching us from afar. They were all talking, laughing and pointing at me.

"It's great to see you after so much time, Derek," said Jesse who was the first to come to me. "Let me introduce the rest of the gang: I'm sure you remember our schoolmates Rodney, Jeanette, Gina, Ina and Ravi. And this is Hannah, Jessica, Tim and Justine."

When he was introducing the people in front of me I was totally speechless. They all looked exactly as they did in high school, they hadn't aged at all. 17-year-old kids. But they radiated much more than that. They looked somehow… happy. And wise. I couldn't explain the feelings that they awoke in me. Like they weren't human in a way.

"Aren't you going to say anything?" Rodney's girlfriend teased me. "Like for example, nice to meet you all...?"

"Of course, nice to meet you," I mumbled. I was till experiencing an emotional cocktail I couldn't exactly explain.

"I think Derek needs to take a rest," said Aaron who had noticed that I seemed totally lost in my own thoughts. The others agreed and said goodbye to the effect of, "See you at home." I was completely in the dark about what they meant with that as well.

*Home? Where is that?* I remembered my rented flat in London. I wondered what the landlord had done with it after I failed to show up for months. And where was I to sleep that night? There, in that house? Just like that? Maybe I could find a way to run away during the night...

"So, do you like it here?" Aaron asked me bringing me back from making my plans.

"In New York?"

"Well, I mean in general. In New York, the house we went to... I'm really sorry for my bad manners. I would like to invite you to spend a month or so in my villa.

"Your villa?"

"The big house we went to. It's very comfortable, it's free, food and drink included..."

There was something suspicious about his offer.

"Why?" I asked.

"Because... well, let's not beat around the bush. Because you have certain... abilities."

It sounded like a line from one of the Superman films. "Abilities, huh?" I asked incredulously.

"Abilities that can be very useful for this world. And besides, I might be able to make it possible for you to see your love again..."

I felt the pain in my chest again. Why was he making fun of my feelings in this way? Ching Lan was dead!

"Look at me," he said and held me by the shoulders turning me to face him.

"If it is possible that I look seventeen years old, don't you think other things are possible too? Why would I lie to you?" his words cut into my consciousness like a knife of truth that allows no disagreements.

"Truth is painful only for those that don't like it. Otherwise truth is one of the most beautiful things in the world. Please come with me," he said opening the door to the taxi.

## XVIII. THE BREAKTHROUGH MONTHS

THE PERIOD THAT FOLLOWED CHANGED MY LIFE FOREVER. I was in a state of shock having experienced so many changes in such a short period of time. Not only was I fired by my magazine for not returning their calls but I also lost the girl that I loved more than anybody else in this world. And to top it all, I was declared insane. And finally I ended up with people that were somehow… happy. Now they expected the same thing from me.

And I… somehow developed a split personality. A part of me felt a connection with them. I wanted to be one of them. To smile all the time, to be fast, youthful; I found out they were all masters of martial arts and who knows what else. Sometimes I thought they still kept some secrets away from me that I was never going to learn.

I also went to a couple of their concerts – this time for free, of course. But I was never allowed to stay backstage – they always asked me to check out how the public saw them. Jesse joked many times that I was the only one who could say what the concert is like and how the audience saw them since the others were so busy with stage effects that they couldn't afford to send somebody else to check things out. I wanted to find out how they managed to do all those tricks, which were, to put it mildly, quite unbelievable, but I wasn't successful. However, I knew there had to be a way for me to discover that…

How was it possible for Jesse to appear on one end of the stage and then only a second later he was floating on the opposite side? How was it possible that their movements were in such perfect sync? But above all,

I was fascinated by the martial arts. Rodney and Jesse staged some kind of guitar fight. They were doing kung fu while playing. But everything was happening so fast that it was impossible to see what kind of effects were used and in what way. As far as playing was concerned, it must have been playback, I was sure about that. But the rest... well, it was just too... impossible.

The other side of me slyly observed the scene. I wanted to know more even if that meant I would have to peek somewhere that I shouldn't. I was curious. And nobody was truly on my side. Nobody wanted to comfort me when I was lonely, nobody seemed to understand me. I wanted to understand what was going on.

Sometimes I would secretly listen in on their rehearsal. But I didn't discover anything important. A couple of punches, some words about choreography and that was that. Jesse and Keisha seemed to radiate some kind of maturity and it was clear that they really enjoyed each other's company. Like Ravi and Ina. And Rodney and Jessica.

Seeing them so joyfully happy together I sometimes almost became jealous. I had a feeling that it was they who separated me from my beloved. They prevented me from attending her funeral... But whenever I spoke about that with Aaron, I came across as a negative person. And he was supposed to be the only one who understood me.

We talked a lot. Also because we shared a life experience. It really bothered me how at peace he seemed with everything that had happened to him. How could you ever be happy again if somebody killed the person you loved? But he seemed to radiate peace all the time, and what was more, he wasn't jealous at all when he saw all those happy couples around him. Quite the opposite, he was happy for them.

And finally, my third part. This part was just a silent observer. I felt torn between the first and the second part. On the one hand, I wanted to be like them, but on the other hand, I hated them. Well, I didn't really hate them. I was just jealous. Sometimes I would remember what Ching

Lan and I talked about the evening she died.

That when you envied someone, you were like a criminal. If they hadn't been here, it would have been me. And then you just eliminated the people that were in your way... *Is this emotion really such madness? How am I to get rid of it? Do I even want to be rid of it?*

Aaron was quite persistent with me. He was ready to talk to me as long as it was necessary for me to realize certain things. Whenever I succumbed to my emotions, he'd encourage me to find peace again. That didn't seem too sensible to me. If I felt anger I couldn't really help it.

"That's not true. It's just your reaction. You are not that emotion. It's just a reflection of your body, ego and genetics. It's result of your thoughts which are not real either. What those feelings don't represent in the least, is you. They are not you, you see?" he would tell me like he wanted to explain to me an incredible solution of a wonderful equation. But I didn't think it was wonderful in the least. If I was not my feelings, who was I then?

"This is where all the fun starts. You start discovering your power and your secret abilities. Who are you?"

I found the part, where he mentioned 'secret abilities', interesting. And the rest sounded like beautiful poetry – which you tend to forget almost as soon as you hear it. And so I lived like this for approximately three months.

# XIV. THE RITE

*I WAS SURROUNDED WITH WHITE BEINGS WHOSE BODIES WERE COVERED IN SCALES. They were bigger than me and very shiny. The circle started glimmering when they started passing around a laser-like beam. Soon the beam had been passed around the entire circle. They connected it in the middle and made a sort of a laser platform above my head.*

*This platform was emitting white light that was composed of all the colors of the rainbow. As they slowly started lowering it towards me I felt slight tingling sensation in my head. That sensation turned into vibration and slowly started spreading down my body. When the platform reached my feet, they started raising it again. This procedure was repeated three times.*

*In the end they slowly retracted the beams that were connecting the circle into the platform. Even the beam that was forming the circle was dissolved. Only they remained present. The biggest one approached me.*

*»Finally,« he said. »You know, it took me quite some time to realize how poisonous resentment really was. Let it go, because unimaginably beautiful things may be waiting for you once you open up the curtain of resentment...«*

*"Have I passed the test?" I asked. It was more than obvious that it was about that.*

*He smiled. "Of course. Now you'll finally be able to do what you came here for ..."*

"What are you thinking about?" Aaron asked me when I awoke from my dream.

"Nothing really. It was just a dream," I replied.

Suddenly he seemed really interested. He looked at me like he already knew what I dreamed about. He asked me seriously.

"What dream?"

"Oh, pure fiction. I dreamed about some white creatures that were testing me with some kind of a laser platform. As I said, nothing special."

"Did you talk?" he wanted to know.

"Yes, we did. Well, the biggest one spoke. But why do you want to know all…?"

"What did he say?" he interrupted me.

"He said that I had passed some kind of test. I don't know really. It sounded logical in the dream. But now the more I think about it the stranger it all seems. Don't you think?"

He smiled with relief and I didn't know what he meant. "Pretty soon you will know," he said with conviction. "Soon you will learn everything you want to know."

I was obviously about to learn everything.

## XX. THE TRUTH REVEALED

H E KINDLY INVITED ME TO GO TO MY ROOM. "Get settled in. Take as much time as you need," he said and closed the door behind him.

Of course I was curious why he was being so mysterious. I waited for a couple of seconds to hear him walk away. I quietly stepped to the door and opened it. In the round corridor I saw his shadow enter Ravi's room. When he closed the door, I heard laughter. I tiptoed to the door.

"Now he is dreaming about the future. This is the second time," said Aaron. "We all know why Derek is so important. He is the only one among us with the ability to…"

I heard a muffled "Shhhh!"

"So what?" I heard Aaron whisper.

"I must tell him. I'm sure he'll understand," he concluded.

"Sure, like I understood then," smiled Jesse.

"This is different. Although he still has a lot of blockages, he is different. I know that," Aaron replied.

"And if he isn't…?"

"Then he'll just leave. We can't make him stay."

"OK, then. Shall we make a presentation?" asked Jesse and then the door suddenly opened. I was standing there and it was obvious I was caught red-handed. I even had a feeling that they knew I was there the whole time.

"Hi, Derek. Come in, please," Aaron invited me like we had agreed I would wait there. I became a bit less scared and I entered the room. The

191

whole group was there. They were sitting in a circle and they made some room for me too. I waited for epiphany.

"Don't be scared. Please try to remain as calm as possible. Can you do that?"

I nodded. I didn't know what to expect. I sat on the floor and 'tried to relax', as instructed. The whole room was filled with silence. Suddenly there was a thought in my head. This surprised me so much that I flinched. It felt like somebody was setting the right radio frequency.

*Derek? Can you hear me?* I heard Aaron's voice ask.

I opened my eyes. Aaron was sitting on the other side of the room with his eyes closed. I went back to my previous sitting position and tried to relax again.

*Derek?* I heard the voice again. I decided to simply try to answer with a thought.

*Yes?*

*You see, you can do it!* he encouraged me. *You just need to be on the right thought frequency. At the moment I'm helping you with this.*

*What do you mean?*

*You will learn the details later,* he replied. *Today I'd like to show you something you have been curious about since you came here. How the stage effects during the concerts are made and why. The answer is simple: to attract as many people as possible. Why as many as possible? Because by listening to our music they could learn to understand the messages that will play a crucial role in the future for saving humanity. You are a very important piece of that puzzle, Derek. And that's why I ask you to try to watch what you are about to witness in a… grounded way.*

*OK. I'll do my best.*

*Are you sure?*

*Yes, I'm sure,* I thought impatiently. At least now I knew why I had a feeling that Aaron was answering my thoughts so many times. Obviously he must have really heard them. Really. After all I had been through, I almost got used to it.

*OK. You'll witness the secret of our teleportation. Please open your eyes.*

I opened my eyes and Keisha was sitting in front of me. She extended her arm and I held her hand. She motioned for my other hand too and I was now holding her right hand with both of my hands. Then something amazing happened: suddenly her right hand sort of melted and I saw Keisha on the other end of the room. Now Jesse was sitting in front of me. I was completely blown out of my mind but I decided to remain sitting. I wanted to create an impression that I was not afraid.

Jesse did a similar thing. The only difference was that he held my left hand with his right hand and twisted them in the way that we ended up holding each other's shoulders. It seemed almost impossible to get out of this 'embrace'. But again he seemed to melt away and soon he was standing on the other side of the room. Now Ina was sitting in front of me. She hugged me and I did the same. A similar procedure followed. She disappeared and reappeared opposite me in the circle.

I looked around and I saw that everybody was satisfied with my seemingly calm reaction. I was still trying to find out if maybe a laser had been hidden anywhere and at the same time I tried to grasp what Aaron wanted to tell me.

*Such abilities will soon become widely used and completely normal*, continued the voice in my head. *You receive them depending on how much you manage to cleanse yourself*, he emphasized.

*Cleanse yourself?*

*That's right. How much negative energy and emotions you are able to admit to yourself are a part of you and how much courage you have to eliminate them. In this way you cleanse yourself. When we learn this technique, we will be stronger than any external force, stronger than robots and low vibrations. This is the strongest weapon in the world.*

*Weapon?*

*Yes. One of the most important milestones in the history of humanity is about to take place and you have the ability that might save the planet.*

I could hardly wait to find out what that ability was.

*You will learn that during training if you decide to stay with us.*

*Are you kidding? Sure I'll stay here*, I answered quickly.

He smiled obviously relieved like he wanted to say: I told you so. The others clapped and in this way welcomed me as an integral part of the group.

*Finally we don't have to hide anymore*, I heard Keisha's voice in my head. Then everybody except Aaron disappeared and we were left alone in the room.

## XXI. THE POWER OF KNOWLEDGE

IN YEARS THAT FOLLOWED I OFTEN DREAMED OF PEOPLE I KNEW BUT in entirely different circumstances than I'd been used to… I'd been learning in New York for a year, mostly from Aaron. Martial arts caused me the most problems. Probably due to the fact that the vision in my left eye was not as good as that in my right eye. Since for ever. When Aaron threw a right punch, I'd actually manage to defend myself sometimes. But when he threw a left one… That was simply impossible for me. Therefore Aaron postponed martial arts training to a time when I'd be ready.

Often we'd just take a walk and he'd talk about living in accordance with natural laws. How to attain high morals and new capabilities. I took much of that knowledge to heart and discovered that it was truly invaluable. I couldn't imagine living my life in the same old way anymore… And I came to understand perfectly why the band members were always in a good mood. And also what kind of morals one had to have to attain capabilities like theirs. I hadn't succeeded in doing that yet. And it also seemed that I wouldn't for quite some time.

Soon the time came to leave New York. The building of the cities that pursued the new way of life was about to begin. Later I discovered that my new friends were among the first to join the construction project and that they directed all the money they'd earned into it. I felt ashamed of having judged them. When I was buying the tickets for Ching Lan and me that first time, I calculated the band's share of the ticket price and I imagined the band spending their days lounging in beach chairs, sipping cocktails. At least I would've done that. I couldn't even dream of such a huge project being developed… When Aaron and I discussed that I apologized to him. And he just grinned widely.

"For someone who has been living in darkness for so long, judging comes perfectly naturally. You should forgive yourself."

"You don't understand," I rushed. "You need to forgive me."

"There's nothing to forgive," he simply stated.

"I beg your pardon?" I looked at him from under my eyebrows. "I resented you, I called you 'little rich bastards' and God knows what else."

"You and a million others who at that time knew nothing about life…" he continued. "There's nothing to forgive, because you didn't do it on purpose! Can you understand that?"

I couldn't understand how he could be so damn calm about the entire thing. I'd have gone nuts from all the negative energy sent to me by millions. Being judged while doing the only smart and sensible thing in the world – the great mission. The redemption of the world. I'd feel wronged and treated unfairly…

"Stop now, immediately!" Aaron stopped my thoughts.

"You're judging again, haven't you noticed that?"

"Who?" I said ignorantly.

"Yourself. People. You're succumbing to ignorance again. Forgive yourself and decide: it'll be different from now on."

"But how can you be so calm about all this? Why didn't you tell people you were building Cities of Happiness and that in reality you're using your entire capital for the development of the future? Why didn't you throw that in our faces?"

"When you're doing what's right, you're calm," he explained. "And when you're doing the wrong thing, you feel bad. If you want to save somebody from darkness, you have to stand in the light. You mustn't follow people's darkness, because it'll swallow you and then you'll save no one. If I'd shared this – then top secret – information with the people

that were attacking us because of their ignorance, those very people could have endangered the formation of the Cities. The news would have spread through the media and who knows what kind of Cities would rise, if any. This way we'd ignored people wishing us wrong, knowing that they weren't doing it because they actually wanted that. And we knew that the construction of these Cities could save all people."

I became silent. Both of us turned quiet for a while. After a few minutes I broke the silence by asking him:

"How do I rid myself of judging?"

He thought for a while and then said: "Have you ever seen a war movie?"

Of course I have. I used to find them heroic, but with time I began to feel that movies with that sort of vibration suited me less and less. The truth is, again I had no idea where he was going with that question.

"If we are in alignment with what we want, our bodies are healthy. If we are happy and if the energy that fuels us is flowing evenly through our organs, we're healthy. But if we surrender to ignorance, the lower vibration that is very quickly drawn to our physical body, inhabits our organs and then… interesting things happen."

He emphasized those last words.

"The heart that used to be pure love now turns into a war general. That general judges incessantly. Together with lungs, that turn from trust into resentment, from a child into a soldier, they form a perfect couple. The general judges, the soldier kills. That's been happening to you all your life. Your own body is slowly driving you towards the end."

"What?" I was so surprised that I nearly forgot to close my mouth. Even when I thought I was judging Jesse and the band favorably I've been nevertheless slowly killing myself.

"That's right," he was short. "So please stop that. I don't resent you at all. But you have to forgive yourself for a whole bunch of things. I suggest you let it all go. Right now."

It sounded much simpler than it really was. Since I didn't know how to do that I changed the subject.

"Thank you for deciding to accompany me," I replied out of context. That much was true.

I was glad that he decided to accompany me even though he needn't have. The others had already teleported there. He decided – considering that I still hadn't passed my teleportation initiation – to go with me to Australia the classical way. By plane.

"You're welcome," he said meaningfully, noticing how I changed the subject.

## XXII. THE FLIGHT TO AUSTRALIA

WE DIDN'T TALK MUCH AT THE AIRPORT. We routinely placed my suitcases on the conveyor belt, while he didn't have any luggage, just his passport. He obviously didn't need it.

"Everything is waiting for me there," he explained.

After we ate our meals – again without much talking – we boarded the plane. We quickly found our seats. We sat down and prepared for the takeoff. Besides a few instructions regarding the flight nothing unusual happened. Aaron was sitting next to me, closing his eyes from time to time. It looked like he was dozing off but I knew he was actually relaxing.

Suddenly, it struck me. In the very seat I had been feeling pretty great just a few moments ago, I suddenly felt an intense pain in my heart. I felt how wrongly I had been acting all these years. It hit me like a stroke of lightning. I began shaking all over my body, feeling my own weakness. I felt the duality of my personality. Like being God and Devil, good and bad, a cop and a killer at the same time. The tears I had been expecting and missing very much an hour ago now streamed down my cheeks as I was taken over by the realization just how unbalanced and bad person I was. It was because of my messed-up identity that I'd also lost the person I loved. And I wanted to die. Truly.

"Again you're thinking wrongly," Aaron warned me, having opened his eyes quite some time ago. "You're giving in to your emotions. To your own drama which you know is not you."

"I-want-to-die!" I sobbed like a child.

"That's just cleansing, cleansing of the heart," he encouraged me. "Step out of that feeling, that's not you. That's your darkness rising to the surface because of the cleansing of your organs."

I didn't understand anything and I didn't want to. I was shaking all over my body, repeating nonsense.

A flight attendant, who had noticed turning heads in the center of the plane, approached in haste.

"Is everything alright?"

"Yes, yes, everything's fine, nothing to worry about. My friend has some emotional issues – he's afraid of flying." He quickly reassured the flight attendant. She produced a small light-brown bottle.

"Drink this," she said and placed the bottle in the palm of my hand. She also handed me a small plastic cup. But I didn't want to drink – I wanted to die!

"Well, that's almost the same thing," said Aaron and poured me a cup. "Drink."

I drank what I was given and calmed down within a minute.

"The place I wanted to take you to isn't suitable for you just yet," he said. "You'll live quite close to us. You'll join us when you're ready," and softly added: "Jesse was right after all..."

It was harder and harder to follow what he was saying. My surroundings, the passengers in their seats and the plane's interior started to merge into a blur until I finally closed my eyes. I woke up only when we landed.

# XXIII. THE TRANSITION TO CITY OF HAPPINESS

WHEN WE ARRIVED IN SYDNEY HE WOKE ME, "SO, SLEEPING BEAUTY, now we have our last chance to enjoy the last normal city you'll see in your life!"

"What do you mean by 'normal'?"

"Do you see that poster over there?" he said pointing at a jumbo poster of an Assim serving people. "In a year you'll be able to see one in every household. Those who won't have it, will be very outdated."

I thought about the development of technology in the last decade. The same thing happened with computers. And mobile phones. Why not with Assims? But I still wasn't sure what he meant with the expression normal city.

"Up to now a normal city was city where people with different ways of thinking lived together. But soon this will no longer be so. The development of robotics will further accelerate this process. Positive people – this means people who have higher abilities than robots, and other people – those that will work with robots or for them, won't be able to live together anymore. They will live separately. And every class will be happy because they will not hinder the life of the other classes of people. These places will be called 'Cities of Happiness'. These are the cities we've been talking about. When an individual is ready to go to a higher class, they will be summoned to take a test. The rules will be very strict and the passing places will be tightly guarded. These places will exist without any problems for a couple of decades. Until the decision time comes."

"What kind of decisions?"

"I can't tell you that. It won't be us who will decide but beings from other planets. Their decisions will be based on how we behave on planet Earth. But no need to worry about that – we are not quite there yet."

We arrived at our hotel.

"What would you like to see? The Opera House? The Bondi Beach? The Harbour Bridge?"

"Well, actually I'd most like to see a City of Happiness," I replied honestly.

"Are you sure about that? That means no more ordinary life for you," he said looking at me questioningly.

"I'm sure, I've had enough of this life."

We sat in the taxi again and Aaron put our suitcases back in. "Well, OK then, if this is what you really want. But you should know there is no way back."

"I know that," I said decidedly. I really wanted to see that city.

"OK," Aaron said shrugging his shoulders and whispered something to the driver. The driver just smirked and drove off.

Soon we came to a vast expansion of desert. Everywhere I looked I saw only desert. We had left the city behind us and all I could see on the horizon was sand and stones.

*I wouldn't want to have car crash here,* I thought. There was nobody to be seen – only sand and stones. There were no cars either; it looked like we were alone in the world.

After long hours of driving I saw something glittering on the horizon. It looked like a big orb with a hole on the top. Like it was a little cracked at the top. The orb was surrounded by two layers that looked like the layers of an onion. There must have been some space between the two layers but from this distance that was impossible to see. All I could see was that this thing was really huge.

I noticed small white dots rising and falling over the middle dome.

"Special abilities practice," Aaron explained. I could hardly wait to

see that with my own eyes.

When we reached the city we quickly took out our suitcases and the taxi driver drove off. We were left alone in front of a big city door. There was a soldier dressed in white guarding it.

"This man lets people into the City of Happiness. He decides in which circle you should be placed. Later your morals are tested and you are placed accordingly. Bear this in mind. According to your morals."

"Morals?"

"It's a combination of what you know about life and to what extent you are implementing this knowledge in practice," he explained quickly. "That's all I can tell you. We must go now."

Aaron walked up to the guard. They bowed to each other. For a while they just looked at each other and it seemed they were communicating with thoughts. And suddenly the guard made a punching move directed at Aaron's stomach. He moved out of the way artfully like they had practiced that before. Then more punches followed for which Aaron seemed to know in advance.

*This is obviously the password*, I thought. *I'm with him anyway.*

When they were done, they started laughing and speaking in about five different languages I had never heard before. I didn't even know that Aaron spoke so many languages. He never told me that. If I had all this knowledge, I would definitely want to show it to others…

Soon their conversation finished, with laughter, of course. I was glad to see that the guard was in such a good mood. Aaron pointed at me. I waved and became a bit anxious.

When Aaron went through the door I wanted to follow him. But the guard stood in my way.

"I'm with him," I said to the guard. Not so long ago we laughed together. "Aaron! Please help me!" I shouted after him. But he was gone. He was allowed to go in.

The guard kept watching me without saying a word. He looked at me for a while and then punched me in the stomach so hard that I was left breathless.

"I – am – really – with – him," I tried to explain while gesturing with one hand and holding my stomach with the other.

Other punches followed soon and because I was not privy to their secret password they all hit home…

*Aaron… why? Why can't I get in…?* I thought. There was no answer.

When the guard started talking in foreign languages that sounded like gibberish to me. Tears came to my eyes. *I'll never see them again*, I thought. *This is my punishment for everything I've done…*

The guard's mood grew worse by the second. He hit me on the head another time and then spoke in English.

"Lack of knowledge of the principle of life, self-pity, crying, sadness, lack of fitness or a desire for it, no energy or life. Sector Three!"

Two men appeared who were dressed in a similar fashion as the guard. They grabbed me by the shoulders and almost dragged me away. The door leading to Sector Three was in the last onion layer.

*So I guess I belong to the lowest class*, I thought bitterly. Then another Aaron's sentence started ringing in my ears, "Are you sure? There is no coming back…"

*Injustice! Injustice!* kept ringing in my head. But the guards didn't pay attention to my thoughts. They shoved me through the door on which it said Sector Three and shut it behind me.

## XXIV. MY WELCOME TO SECTOR THREE

UPON LANDING ON THE GROUND TOGETHER WITH MY CASES, I QUICKLY looked around to see what was waiting for me, expecting a gang of criminals, murderers or worse. The street that opened up in front of me looked pretty normal. There were houses on either side, the kind you see in some suburbs. Besides the garbage surrounding some houses the city looked pretty normal. I heard a child's voice behind me.

"Do you need help?"

I turned around and saw a nice little girl holding my suitcase.

"Yes, please," I replied quickly. "Actually, I'm not even sure where I'm going..." I started. But she couldn't have been less interested in hearing it. Other kids came from the houses and ran to my things that were all I had – including money and documents – each of them grabbed hold of one item and they disappeared immediately. It took me some time to realize I was left without anything.

Obviously I wasn't wrong about criminals. I took a couple of steps forward to assess the safety of the street. The houses looked really friendly. People were watching TV and they didn't look aggressive at all. I decided to go from door to door until someone invited me in and offered me dinner.

As I knocked on the first door I noticed somebody getting up from the sofa visibly annoyed.

"If this is another sales rep or a religious fanatic, I'll blow their head off!" said the bald man grumpily. He furiously opened the door.

"What do you want?"

I looked at him trying to decide how to explain my problems to him.

"I'm sorry to disturb you," I started politely. "I'm neither a sales rep nor a religious fanatic," I said trying to make a good impression. "I'm just hungry. I've just arrived in Sector Three and I've been robbed…"

"So you're a bum, then! That's even worse! Bloody lying parasites! Get lost or I'll blow your lying head off!" he kept shouting. Not wanting any trouble I went away immediately. I said "Good night!" and went away. I was happy to see that he soon closed his door without getting his shotgun out.

When I came to the next house I tried to assess the owner in advance. A nice façade, flowers on windowsills. I could say I was a sales person and maybe they would offer me at least a biscuit. I was really starving by now. I didn't think it was a good idea to eat anything when Aaron and I arrived because I expected a big dinner in City of Happiness. I just didn't know I wasn't going to be invited.

I rang the bell and an old lady opened the door. The door chain moved only so much that I could see the owner's face which looked at me in a suspicious manner.

"Good evening, dear lady," I started pleasantly. "I'm here to offer you some special services for your home. Cleaning, washing, ironing and more, all done in a special fashion. If you let me in and offer me a cookie, I'll be happy to demonstrate all our services." I thought the idea was brilliant.

But the woman quickly replied, "Thank you, but I don't need this," and closed the door before I could protest.

*This will be more difficult than I imagined,* I thought to myself. The more that I thought about my options, the more hopeless the situation seemed. But I decided not to give up. There had to be a way, I kept thinking to cheer myself up. Just had to.

The evening soon became night as I tried my luck in about twenty more houses. But they were all just versions of the first two. To make things worse, a gang of teenagers attacked me, beat me up and took the few things I had in my pockets. But I was pretty glad they let me live… Soon I gave up looking for a warm place to stay and fell asleep lying on the endless sandy path between the suburban houses.

## XXV. LIFE IN SECTOR THREE

"**R**ONNIE, HAND ME A LOG!" I shouted as I emptied the container. Soon my colleague and friend Ronnie started handing me the logs that would form somebody's new home.

He was the only person in this world I could talk to and get on with. But he was a robot. I didn't see this as shameful. The people in Sector Three were unstable and unreliable. But Ronnie the robot took me in on my second day in Sector Three. That was five years ago. We became true friends, as true as a friendship with a robot can be. I told him everything about myself and he shared some details with me too – who made him, when he was activated and other things. He always acted as I expected and he never stole or treated me unfairly in any other way. We established a rather idyllic relationship.

He helped me not to get beaten or robbed everywhere I went and he also arranged a job for me so that I could take responsibility over my life again. It was the first time in my life that I worked really hard for a living and actually felt pretty proud of that.

He also helped me with my eye problem. He showed me a special exercise that helped me improve sight in my left eye.

"It's only a matter of anatomy," he explained simply. "What moves the eye is a muscle. Sort of like my circuitry. If you believe this to be true, you can train it. Like fitness. In this way you can get rid of your system error that is connected with your fear of seeing something."

It was as he said. With exercising I managed to eliminate my 'system error'. Ronnie was pretty strict about exercising and I was really grateful to him when we succeeded and I was now better equipped for learning martial arts, what he was teaching me too. I was amazed about how many programs he had and soon I respected him like he was a human being.

I also admired him because I was able to learn from him how to react. He was immune to people's stupidity. Because he was incapable of emotions, he was not upset when he saw an injustice being done or our neighbors' insane behavior. He simply knew that people who got angry were damaged.

"Damaged program," he said. I felt better immediately.

Holidays with him were something special too. Christmas, New Year, Easter. He had plenty of recipes and we could get as creative as we wanted. He helped me very much at the time when I needed someone to talk to. We analyzed all my life experiences and resentments. I told him everything from my childhood onwards. About how three classmates and me formed a dancing group in primary school and how one day they decided they wanted to continue without me. They went to a talent competition as a trio and won. They became one of the most recognizable dancing groups in the country. Then about how I courted this girl at a party and how later on she became a successful model. About my high school classmate who suddenly became famous and how his concerts are sold out months in advance. We talked about envy and resentment. How this patterns seemed to follow me around all my life.

When he explained his (robot's) point of view, I was really amused. He spoke about programs and how it was my choice what I wanted to keep on my hard drive. He had his own unique view on each matter.

I really had fun in his company. I was really glad that it was impossible for me to hurt him. I couldn't offend him and I couldn't harm him. I understood why the development of Assims was so important for people. To take a load off our shoulders. Human company was of course still a priority for me but unfortunately there was absolutely no one I could

spend time with in Sector Three. My criteria for company were very high. One day a service guy knocked on our door and said that Ronnie had to go to a workshop. There seemed to be a problem with his circuitry. We said goodbye and it was the first time that I noticed Ronnie's electronics to blink funnily.

"He has grown attached to you," explained the service guy. "He got used to your frequency and it would be very hard for him to function without it. Such a program has to be recycled because it is no longer functional for others."

I wasn't exactly sure what he was trying to tell me but somehow I gathered he wanted to kill Ronnie. I tried to prevent that but he threatened me by telling me that there was a jail in Sector Three too.

"And believe me, you don't want that experience," he said angrily while dragging my only friend away. In an hour or so, people who claimed they lived in the house Ronnie and I had lived in for five years, came and forcefully threw me out.

I was angry and very confused.

*Why is this happening to me? And why now when I really started to enjoy living here,* I thought. I stopped. Joy. Happiness. Satisfaction. These emotions were in accordance with natural laws. Aaron's words came back to me.

*"Here your morals are evaluated and you are transferred accordingly. Bear this in mind. According to your morals."*

*"Morals?"*

*"It's a combination of what you know about life and to what extent you are implementing this knowledge in practice."*

Maybe it was all just a test. Maybe I was prepared to be placed in a higher sector. Maybe I had learned something in five years…

*I must try to be happy; I mustn't give in to the feelings of despair again. Not now when maybe I'm quite close to obtaining new abilities. To become free.*

## XXVI. THE TEST

I STOOD IN FRONT OF THE HOUSE AND STARTED TO LAUGH. There must have been a reason I had to spend so much time in Sector Three. I always had a feeling that I was somehow different than other people. There was some hidden part of my personality that made me too dangerous to learn more about Jesse and the rest of them.

I wanted to be one of them but obviously still didn't master enough of their knowledge. Now I was standing in front of the house watching the sky. It started to get cloudy and the first raindrops began falling on my face. Soon the cloud seemed to tear up completely and it started pouring. Since I was homeless I thought it would be a good idea to at least get a good wash.

I took off my shirt enjoying the summer rain. The thought how beautiful and mysterious life was, brought a smile on my face. I knew I was in trouble but I considered that to be a challenge. I wondered how I was going to get out of this scrape. And I became amused. I washed and started to whistle.

Then a policeman came up to me.

"What are you doing, sir?" he asked.

"What does it look like I'm doing? I'm washing," I said and smiled.

"Do you happen to have some soap and a towel maybe?" I inquired.

"This is an outrage! Of course I don't have soap and towel! Please come with me immediately."

*Great,* I thought. *I won't be sleeping under the stars tonight.*

The policeman led me along narrow streets to a small police station. I stepped into the lobby which was divided into two parts. To the left it said 'Jail' and to the right 'Sector Two'. He directed me to the right, opened a small door and pushed me in. There were five people sitting in the room. They looked like some sort of panel of judges. There were three young men dressed in dark blue clothes and similarly dressed two women.

When I entered they asked me if I knew why I was here. I answered.

"I'm here to learn it's all just a test. I cannot blame anyone for anything, because all the people surrounding me are there just to make me see my own darkness which I need to overcome. Everything, really everything is a test. I know that now. I needed five years to finally realize that."

They looked at each other and began a discussion. Although nobody said a word I knew they were trying to decide what to do with me.

"All right," said an older female member of the team. "If you manage to get through that door, you're accepted to Sector Two. Good luck!"

I looked in the direction that she showed to me and I found out I was just a couple of yards away from the light blue door. It looked too simple to be true.

*Things are not always as they seem*, I thought. So I really focused as I made the first step towards the door. I was glad I had prepared myself because a surprise followed.

Two men appeared in my way and prevented me to continue. My head started to buzz. I didn't know what it was but it sounded like a radio frequency.

*From the left*! I heard a man's voice say. At that moment a blow hit me from the left and I fell to the floor. It hit me in the ribs so it took me quite a while to catch my breath again. It was strong and precise. The men didn't want to hurt me or break my ribs deliberately. The punch was exactly as strong as I could take to be able to get up again and fight.

*He will get up*, I heard a voice say again.

*I think he managed to make the connection*, the other one thought.

*It was about time*, added a woman's voice. *The credit goes to the robot. Ronnie really did a tremendously good job.*

I looked around the room and saw the commission exchanging glances and smiles. Similar to the time when Aaron was communicating with the guard. At that time I didn't understand their communication. Now it seemed much easier. If they told me from which direction I could expect a blow to come, it would be much easier, of course. I was better prepared now.

The two men were still standing in front of me.

*The legs!* I heard a voice say again. I leapt into the air and at the same time one of the men delivered an extremely fast kick directed into the space where I had stood a moment ago. If I hadn't heard the warning, I would have ended up on the ground again.

*Well, that's better,* they thought. What followed then was a training that looked like a computer game. They would announce each punch or kick before they carried it out.

Upper left! Right – ribs! Straight ahead – leg! Head – from the side! Side arch!

And I kept dodging them. But soon I grew tired of that too. This allowed me to survive but I wasn't getting any closer to the door. I realized I would have to change my tactics.

I started to attack. But they must have been able to hear my frequency too. They seemed to know exactly what I was going to do. So they fought off every kick or punch that I delivered. We exchanged moves for a while like in a game of chess. I was completely sweaty by this time, but I still had no idea how to get to the door...

If they were reading my mind, they knew exactly which punches I was going to throw. *How could I surprise them?* I thought. I saw them smiling and I knew they were able to read this thought too...

*No thoughts,* I heard their answer. Was it really possible – were they helping me?

*Of course,* answered one of them. *It's all just a test. Why shouldn't we help somebody who was trying to pass it? You're connected with us.*

*So. Without thoughts,* I thought. I defended myself from their punches and soon started to hear silence in my head... I realized they had stopped

thinking about how to attack me. I kept falling to the ground again.

*That's not fair*, I thought.

*This is a test*, was the answer. I didn't give up. I got up. Without any thoughts. When did I have no thoughts? When I was sleep? It seemed logical. I prepared my body for the fight and at the same time decided to prepare my mind for sleep. Each decision that I made would be a reflection of something other than my decision. I will let myself be guided by something bigger than myself. I felt my body being consumed by that special sweet feeling you normally get just before falling asleep. My mind started to descend into some sort of alpha state while my body was still ready for the fight.

I made a step towards them and with a part of my consciousness I saw that they started to attack me. I surrendered my body to the same force that was leading them. No thoughts… I felt silence like during sleep but my body kept fighting and it seemed I was able to observe it winning. I became very fast. Faster than ever before. Although there were two attackers, I was able to see the whole development of the fight in advance. I had to make sure to stay relaxed and prevent my state of mind, which seemed so easy to maintain now, not to drive me into narcissism.

My body jumped and I managed to knock them down with my legs. Now it was the first time that it was they who fell to the ground. I reached towards the doorknob. The girl, who I had just seen sitting at the table, appeared in front of me. She took my hand and gently spun me in the air and again I landed on the ground. Now I had to fight three people. If I wanted to defeat them I not only had to fight without any thoughts but also increase my energy levels.

When I was able to move out of my head, a part of me just followed the situation. It looked like a kung fu film. And a bit like ballet. Soon I was able to find a way to defeat all three of them. When I reached for the doorknob this time, I wasn't surprised when I saw the other two members of the panel.

When I was fighting all five members I had to collect all my strength to remain calm. I felt a strong wave of something thick, bright and bigger than me run through my body like the electric current. I became very fast and soon I wasn't even following my own blows, I just surrendered to the energy guiding me.

I saw the outcome of the fight in advance. I felt I really loved the people I was fighting with. I knew they wanted only what was best for me. This feeling filled me with new strength. The friendship I felt for them, the happiness that was overflowing me like a giant wave and the silence inside my head, like I had never experienced before, made me begin to feel who I really was.

I wasn't really who I had wanted so hard to be all my life. I was not a success-starved freak envious of everyone. I was total peace. I really wanted what was best for people. Because I had so much power in me I also had a lot of darkness that I had to overcome. It was only that.

Feeling totally at peace, which I enjoyed so much, I turned around my axis and knocked down all five of my opponents. I dashed towards the door, reached for the knob and opened it. Nobody followed me to stop me. When I opened the door, the others got off the ground gallantly and joined hands in front of them. They bowed to me and I could hear their thought.

*Congratulations for passing the test. Have a pleasant stay in Sector Two.*

## XVII. MY REAL WELCOME

WHEN I ENTERED I NOTICED THAT THE WALL SEPARATING THE two sectors was actually one of those big shells around the orb that I saw five years ago when Aaron and I looked at the city from the outside. From Sector Three you couldn't even see that wall so well. Because like an onion layer, it was facing the other layer – Sector Two, it was visible only from the inside, that means from where I was standing now. I knew I was in the middle between the two and I was glad that I had obviously passed the test.

The city that opened up in front of me was much bigger than the previous one. The other city was oblong in shape and it spread around Sector Two. The walls were so high and smooth that they were impossible to climb over.

This city was wider. Obviously there were more people living here or they just needed more space. The houses were light and open, there were many round shapes. There were no locks on the doors and I noticed some kind of mutual trust. The people smiled a lot and were very open. If you were able to pass a test like mine, you obviously knew it paid to maintain the state of happiness at all times.

A young boy who looked like an Asian warrior approached me.

"Welcome to Sector Two, Derek," he greeted me with a smile. "My name is Chang and I'm here to accompany you. I guess you want to know where you'll be living, right? Please follow me."

I was really surprised how well I was accepted. I followed him and subconsciously still expected to run into gangs of robbers and street fighters at every street corner. When you'd lived in such environment for five years, you simply got used to that.

"This doesn't exist here anymore," he said smiling. "Happiness is standard here. People are well aware that it's in their best interest to act according to the laws of nature. But their morals are not yet high enough to develop special abilities. They don't know that they have fantastic powers hidden inside of them that are totally beyond their expectations. The goal of this sector is to realize that life is a challenge."

"That's it?" I asked.

"Well, yes, that's it. But you really need to… *realize* that. You need to believe it and really live it."

It sounded so simple.

He looked at me one more time to emphasize the seriousness of his statement. "Some people stay here to the end of their lives not knowing that they don't really have to die."

This news surprised me too. Everyone dies. That was a natural cycle of life.

"It's not necessary. You can develop your body to reach its full potential. Well, I could speak to you about that for years on end. Here we are," he said pointing at a big building whose edges were slightly rounded, with the doors and windows of the same shape. It looked like an enormous flower bud.

"Do you like it?" he asked me.

"Sure I do," I said and remembered my previous home that was of a considerably lower standard. I slowly began to realize that the people in this sector got on so well here because they felt safe.

"Sometimes you can be demoted to Sector Three exactly for that," my escort smiled.

"What do you mean? Aren't the people who have passed the test…"

"Able to stay here forever? No. If you become too complacent and are no longer prepared to develop, you can easily be sent back. People sometimes don't know why that happens. One day they simply wake up on the other side of the wall."

*This must be quite a shock*, I thought. I took my new things that had been brought to me and moved into my new house.

## XVIII. SECTOR TWO

PEOPLE IN SECTOR TWO WERE REALLY TOTALLY DIFFERENT FROM THOSE living in Sector Three. They maintained the state of happiness all the time. Later I discovered that was the condition for living there. There were cameras placed all over the city and if you were caught in a bad mood more than five times, you were questioned by a special committee and accused of 'contaminating others with your negative energy'. I was caught about three times, but that was at the very beginning.

It was interesting that in Sector Two money didn't exist anymore, so what I made in Sector Three I could just as well throw away. There were shops and the shops assistants used lasers to record what people would take but that was only to know what was running out and what they had to order.

There were people of different races and ages like in Sector Three. On the south part of the city there was a well-maintained cemetery. The city was clean all the time and the doors of the houses were left unlocked at all times. People moved freely in the city and everyone had their purpose. The people were very creative in various fields – architecture, arts and sciences. Children went to specific schools where they received needed education. People in this sector meditated a lot and believed that each test was a challenge.

I got a job that was a reflection of my abilities. On my second day there, Chang took me to an office where I was asked what I had done before in my life.

"I wrote," I told them.

They looked at each other and I felt they weren't too happy to hear that. And then another question followed.

"What did you write?"

"Mostly tourist articles. But I want to write a book..." I went on although I felt that writing a bestseller was no longer my top priority.

"Are you aware that writing books is... outdated?" an older member of the commission asked me.

"What do you mean?"

"I mean it's much better to live your life than to write about it. That's why we try to avoid reading and writing books in Sector Two."

"Oh," I said quickly. This was what I had felt in myself earlier. I was gradually growing so consumed by life itself that it didn't seem to make sense to write about it anymore. But my wish to really live my life was growing bigger and bigger. That 'bestseller' would just have to wait for my next life.

"What else can you do?" an older man asked me.

"I can do... martial arts, I can talk to people... I can exist without thoughts."

These abilities made much bigger impression on them than the ones I mentioned before. I was given a task of training teenagers who had finished primary education. Similar to high school gym class. Initially that seemed much too broad for me. I was afraid I wasn't going to be able to do it. But soon I calmed down and embraced the challenge.

As it turned out the task was actually right up my alley since the teenagers in Sector Two had very little in common with teenagers in ordinary cities and Sector Three. We had regular practices to keep fit and strong and I taught them how to fight without using the mind. Since I was able to read the mind of each of them, they had to try really hard to defeat me. I was really surprised how powerful I was becoming. I didn't even know since when I had been able to read minds so well. This skill seemed to become stronger in me with every lesson I gave to my students. Soon

I was able to tune into the frequency of thoughts even when I was not in a fight. I knew that this tuning in was intended only for good things and not for eavesdropping.

I soon became aware of the fact that I would be turning forty pretty soon. Life in Sector Two was so overwhelming that I had completely lost track of time. I remembered Chang who said that some people spent their entire lives here. And soon something happened that made me realize the huge difference between my life here and the life I had had before. But this knowledge came with a sting...

# XXIX. THE VISIT

"**Y**OU HAVE A VISITOR," SAID CHENG WHEN I ASKED HIM WHY HE WAS waiting for me by the lawn where we had our training.
I thought it quite incredible that somebody would want to visit me here. I was planning to go back to get my dad because I knew he could really benefit from this knowledge, taking into account the changes we were about to go through.

"And... who is it?" I asked carefully.

"You'll see pretty soon. Just make sure you don't succumb to sadness. Remember that everything is just a test, or even better, a challenge," he said handing me a bracelet made of symmetrical stones of different colors. Each of them had an engraved map and when I looked closely I realized it would be impossible to make a copy because the engravings were made so meticulously.

"This bracelet is a proof that you live in Sector Two. So you can return easily. If you manage to maintain the state of happiness of course."

I didn't know what he meant. Like I was facing another test. And I was right.

A doorman took me to the exit from Sector Two along a small snake-like tunnel. I even recognized the room in which I was when I was sent to Sector Three all those years ago. Knowing it was all just a memory I smiled feeling relived.

The postman was waiting at the front door. Having been used to the life in Sector Two, seeing a postman like they used to be once, was quite an experience. He wasn't aware of that, of course. He was just doing his job which obviously still existed in the old cities. Probably in Sector

Three too. Sectors Two and One surely didn't need him anymore. He was standing at the front door and I could see that he was waiting for me.

*So this is my big test*, I thought relieved.

"Derek Blake?" he asked quickly. "You've got a registered letter."

I signed the piece of paper he prepared for me and playfully realized how that reminded me of my old life. The only things missing were my morning robe and a cup of coffee in my hand. That's how I used to answer the front door and sign for the mail in the mornings.

He thanked me and left. He drove away in an SUV. Obviously here even postmen had vehicles that enabled them to cover larger distances. Back home, in England, he'd have driven away on a bicycle or a motor scooter.

I held the envelope in my hand for a moment and then opened it. I could feel a slight uncertainty when I found out it was a letter. Who could possibly have sent me a letter?

*Dear Derek,*

*I'm sorry you have to find out about it this way… If you're reading this, I'm dead. Don't rack your brain about the funeral; I shall be buried among my people in Africa. I just wanted to say that I sometimes regret not having seen more of you, my son. I probably haven't shown enough interest in you, in where you are and what you're doing. It was too hard being a good father after your mother's death, because every detail in your face reminded me of her… Please forgive me for that.*

*This is obviously a goodbye… Don't come to Africa, because you won't find me. Carry me in your thoughts and your heart. Please, remember me as a good father. To me you've always been a good son. It doesn't matter how successful or unsuccessful you think you are.*

*I love you.*

*Your father,*

*Jim Blake*

It seemed odd and official that he added his own name. But that name was the proof that the letter was indeed meant for me.

I slowly let go of the letter and it dropped to the ground with a soft whisper. Then the wind blew and an air current suddenly lifted it high above my head. As I watched it disappearing in the sky I suddenly regretted letting it go. That was the only document regarding my father that I had. The only proof that he loved me...

I realized how much I'd wanted him to tell me that before he died. His simple life that used to seem so insignificant to me had ended now. I realized that I didn't have anybody else in this world anymore and a hollow feeling of sadness washed over me.

Would he have lived had I invited him to me, to the City of Happiness? He probably would. Thinking that my heart smarted.

Of course he'd have lived, because he'd have led an entirely different life! With me he'd have learned everything that Ronnie the robot would have told us. He'd have made the transition to Sector Two with me and we'd have gotten to know each other much better. He'd have never ever ended up on the other side of the planet, in a forsaken forest, not knowing even where I was.

I regretted not having him by my side. Not inviting him with me. Back then I hadn't even thought of him. And now that very thing seemed so important! I remembered what he had written in the letter... To me you've always been a good son...

I smiled through my tears and suddenly the view of the desert changed.

Three members of the panel that assessed me before I entered Sector Two materialized in front of me. The woman came closer.

"Are we breaking the rules, Derek?"

"Excuse me?"

"The feelings of sadness are filling up your mind," she explained. "Do you want to return to Sector Two or do you want to go back to Sector Three?" she asked calmly.

I wiped my tears off. I didn't want to go back but I also wasn't feeling as happy as I had before. I showed her my bracelet and headed to the door.

"You will come back when you are ready," she said and disappeared behind the door. Once again I was left standing in front of the door looking after them. I was at the beginning again.

## XXX. THE DOORMAN

"WELL, NOT REALLY AT THE VERY BEGINNING," I HEARD A DEEP voice say.
I turned around and I saw the big guard who had sent me to Sector Three years ago.

"The only thing you need is my permission," he added. "I can see that you've made a big progress in recent years," he said sounding important.

I certainly didn't feel that. I fought with feelings of sadness and guilt, and I thought it was all my fault.

"Maybe you're right," the doorman interrupted my train of thought. "I made a mistake."

Only now did I begin to realize what he had tried to tell me before. If I stayed here, I would never be able to repair anything. Another one of Aaron's sentences came to me: "Derek has the ability to save us all."

What if he was right? What if such an ability was really hidden inside of me? An ability that could neutralize my negative pole and give me back the two people that meant the most to me? Was that *really* possible? Were they right? My heart started to beat more soundly at the thought that maybe I was really able to change some things. All I had to do was discover who I really was. I turned to the guard one more time.

"I've changed my mind. I really wish to go back in."

"That's the spirit," he said and smiled. "Go right ahead!"
"What about the test...?" I said cautiously.

"Why should you take the test twice when obviously you are mature enough to get through the door?" he said smiling.

I went past him. My steps were hurried as I walked by – in case he changed his mind.

When I got home I remembered my friends from ten years ago and discovered that it was my firm goal to find them. Not knowing how to get from Sector Two to Sector One I decided to look for Chang. And I was right. He knew the answers to all my questions.

# XXXI. THE TRANSITION

»THE TRANSITION TO SECTOR ONE IS CONSIDERED TO BE IMPOSSIBLE by many. There is no door leading there, nor any other type of passage. You have to be highly moral and very courageous to take such a journey.«

»Journey? I thought the whole time that Sector One was hiding behind the next wall…«

»Of course it is,« he was trying to explain. »But the road there might be a little longer than it seems at first sight. And to get there you have to have… very special abilities.«

This beating around the bush was becoming slightly tiresome. I really wanted to learn the facts.

»How do I get there?«

»You have to pay a visit to the city commission and ask them for a challenge. In Sector Two the city residents have to realize for themselves that they want to advance to a higher level. Nobody can compel them to do that. That's why many stay here for the rest of their lives. Because they're too comfortable here.«

After several years I finally discovered the purpose of this sector. I must've been fond of the comfort myself, or else I wouldn't have stayed here so long. I went home and spent some time preparing for the challenge in front of me. I packed a few things I thought I'd need on the long journey that Chan described. A small and practical tent that set up by pressing the button, some hiking equipment and some food. I crammed everything into a backpack.

Since I didn't know how long this journey would last, I decided to take good care of my personal hygiene. I shaved and looked at myself in the mirror. I'd changed quite a bit in the past ten years. I grew from a boy into a mature man. During my high school years, forty seemed like a really old age. Now that I was that age it seemed even worse than all those years ago. I was still taking care of my physical condition, just like I was teaching my students. But I really didn't enjoy the aging process.

I was so engrossed in my thoughts that I almost forgot about my intention. I splashed my face with cold water again to clear my mind. Then I went to the city commission. They were already gathered and it seemed like I was the one they had been waiting for.

»You probably know why I came here,« I told them as I walked through the door of the large hall. In the middle of it was an oblong desk with five chairs.

»To get a challenge,« they answered and smiled. They obviously weren't used to seeing a lot of people like me.

The commission members closed their eyes and sat still for a while. I was waiting for their decision, wondering what it would be. It looked like they were deliberating. After an hour or so they calmly opened their eyes.

»Very well,« said one of them. »If you can find the exit in this room, you may transfer to Sector One. You know, *everything's a challenge.*«

The commission members got up and vanished into thin air in front of me. I wasn't that surprised, because I'd been witnessing what Jesse and the company had been doing for a long time. I was more puzzled by the fact that suddenly I couldn't see any doors. Everywhere I looked were just walls and no doors.

Firstly, I walked around the room feeling the walls with my hands. Maybe I overlooked something… I found nothing. Secondly, I studied the ceiling and the floor. Again without results. I also became hungry and thirsty.

I was glad that I brought food and snacks with me. Yet I had a weird premonition that my supplies probably wouldn't last until I found the exit. The commission members left and it seemed like they weren't coming back. And the hall really had… no exit.

I decided to continue searching and try to economize on food and drink as much as possible. The first day I checked all the walls and the floor approximately two hundred and fifty times. I'd knock on the marble tiles covering the floor and listen for the hollow sound beneath… I knocked on every single one of the ten thousand three hundred and twenty-two of them. I discovered nothing.

The second day I repeated the whole process. I was much more tired than the day before. Probably because I could feel that feeling the walls and knocking on tiles wouldn't bring me the desired solution. I had food for just a couple of days more.

On the third day I added banging on and kicking the walls to my search. And I soon started screaming for help. Nothing more rational came to my mind. Since I didn't have much more time left, I tried to take advantage of any available possibility. Including the one to go back to where I was before. I really didn't want to die in that large hall.

Soon after I fell to the ground from exhaustion and realized that no one was coming, I seriously started searching for the way out of this place. I realized that so far I was merely trying to find the way out. I was trying to the best of my abilities.

*I don't care about my best abilities,* I thought, *if they don't get me out of here. I need to get more creative!*

I could feel that I wasn't going to help myself by giving up and giving in to the feeling of hopelessness I was experiencing. I sat down and started meditating. I was thinking about how something inside me was preventing me from rising to the challenge. I thought of Aaron and how easily he had made the transition. Even though after many years of living in Sectors Three and Two I managed to abandon many negative emotions, I realized that I still resented him… He was really my true friend. And he obviously wanted me to face all this.

*I can't and I mustn't stay here or I'll die,* I thought. *Do I really want my life to end in this hall? No – the future is positively bright. I have to find the exit. I have to let all the stupid things from my past go.*

I saw myself as a comical marionette that I wasn't and never had been even remotely in control of. I had always been led by the knowledge – or the lack of it.

*I'll surely find the way out,* I thought.

Absolutely nothing happened for about an hour. I was sitting still, trying to connect to the flow that was usually guiding me during the fights. Soon I experienced a absolute relaxation of every single muscle in my body. Despite that I felt more prepared for an attack by the second. Total wakefulness and total relaxation at the same time. I could also feel that I wasn't alone. The room suddenly seemed full of people. Full of beings, to be exact. I decided to open my eyes and see for myself what was going on.

I was surrounded with white beings whose bodies were covered in scales. They were bigger than me and very shiny. The circle started glimmering when they started passing around a laser-like beam. Soon the beam had been passed around the entire circle. They connected it in the middle and made a sort of a laser platform above my head.

This platform was emitting white light that was composed of all the colors of the rainbow. As they slowly started lowering it towards me I felt slight tingling sensation in my head. That sensation turned into vibration and slowly started spreading down my body. When the platform reached my feet, they started raising it again. This procedure was repeated three times.

In the end they slowly retracted the beams that were connecting the circle into the platform. Even the beam that was forming the circle was dissolved. Only they remained present. The biggest one approached me.

»Finally,« he said. »You know, it took me quite some time to realize how poisonous resentment really was. Let it go, because unimaginably beautiful things may be waiting for you once you open up the curtain of resentment...«

»Have I passed the test?« I asked. It was more than obvious that it was about that.

He smiled. »Of course. Now you'll be finally able to do what you came here for.«

»Where do I go now?« I asked.

»Now you're ready. Think of where you want to be and your new body will take you there,« he answered. Soon after that the group vanished into thin air.

I was still sitting on the floor. When the silence of the hall I was sitting in engulfed me, I thought for a moment that I might have been dreaming about everything. It seemed so familiar… I opened my eyes and discovered that I was dressed completely differently than before. Instead of hiking pants and a shirt I was wearing some sort of a white outfit. The pair of pants that resembled jeans and the white t-shirt I was wearing definitely weren't mine. At least they hadn't been before.

I looked once more around the room and came to the same conclusion that nothing in it had changed except my clothes. I looked up and down my body again and realized with great surprise that besides my clothes my appearance had also changed. I reached into my backpack where I had a lot of requisites. A practical small mirror among other things. I could use it for directing the light, but this time I simply looked into it.

My body looked… new. Regenerated. I looked like a teenager. There were no traces of a forty-year-old teacher left. I was just Derek once again. Anyhow, during my time in different sectors of City of Happiness so many unbelievable things had happened that I should have been used to them by now.

I remembered my goal again and put the mirror away. I sat on the floor and thought about Sector One… What it must look like… Probably green. With round architecture. And blue sky.

*Sector One. I want to get into Sector One.* I relaxed again and connected with the familiar flow… *Sector One. Sector One.*

My body completely surrendered to the new vibration and I soon didn't see, hear or feel anything anymore. I was engulfed by the light and before I knew it I felt the softness of grass under me.

# XXXII. THE MEETING

**»D**EREK, WE'VE JUST BEEN TALKING ABOUT YOU,« SAID JESSE. I opened my eyes and realized that I was sitting encircled by my friends. They were peacefully sitting around me in a big blooming meadow. A little girl was sitting next to Ravi and Ina. And a three-year-old boy next to Jesse and Keisha. When I smiled at them they all cheerfully applauded. I made it.

We got up and hugged each other.

»These are Zyna and Kairon,« said Ina and instructed the children to introduce themselves. They were incredibly beautiful and smiling.

I was deeply touched as I took another look at the group I hadn't seen all these years. I'd missed them.

»And how we've been missing you,« said Aaron. »Each year I counted the seconds leading up to your enlightenment. But – it doesn't matter, you're here now.«

I hugged each and every one of them with sincere joy and then took a look around me.

Sector One reminded me of paradise. There were a lot of meadows that were simply heavenly. Everything was surrounded by the round architecture that reminded me of science-fiction movies. Everything matched perfectly. When I looked up in the sky I discovered that people were actually able to fly in Sector One. Without any help. They were moving either by teleportation or flying. The incredible sight spread in front of me was further enhanced by something unusual, almost archaic: the residents of Sector One who wanted to consume food produced it by themselves. Round buildings were surrounded with varicolored small gardens where people were talking to the plants, singing to them and laughing around them, like they would in the company of another person. Aaron sensed what I was astonished with.

»If you grow vegetables the right way – by soaking seeds in saliva and taking into account the alignment of planets during the planting, you get your own pharmacy that surpasses any of those high-tech ones. Local residents are well aware of all the riches our planet is providing,« he explained.

»Let's get to work now,« he changed the subject.

"Work?" I was confused. It also appeared that time had stopped in this sector. It didn't seem to me that people were under stress or buried in work.

*Did you think we didn't work here?* joked Jesse. *On the contrary, we work even harder than elsewhere. And the challenges are much bigger.*

We went to our big house where everybody had their own compartment to live in. These houses didn't have stairs or elevators. The floors were open, like in a beehive. Everybody could fly or teleport themselves wherever they wanted to.

Aaron called a meeting that same afternoon.

*I know some of you are pretty new around here, but we are rather in a hurry,* he thought when we gathered.

*I think we all agree that the situation is pretty critical.*

I didn't know what he meant by that.

*I'll show you,* thought Aaron seriously. *Please, close your eyes.*

I closed my eyes and my consciousness was overflowed with images that weren't mine. It was the same as thought transfer, only when images were being transferred, the energy was much more compacted. To be able to see what was surrounding me, I had to relax. If I tried to sharpen the images forcibly, they'd disperse into a haze again. Like with Ronnie's eye exercises.

I managed to tune in to the frequency of Aaron's images and realized that they were movies showing fighting. Millions of people were shouting like crazy and running towards Cities of Happiness. They were accompanied by dark shadows and it was more than obvious that these people somehow weren't themselves. They seemed more like artificially bred animals trained to obey orders.

*That's what they are,* thought Jessica horrified. *I could've been one of them…*

Rodney put his arm around her shoulders.

I looked at Aaron. *What did she mean by that?*

*These are controlled people, Derek. During the years you spent in City of Happiness, things on the outside changed radically. Do you remember me telling you were in a normal city for the last time? In the city of mixed people? I was right. In the following years happiness became a standard elsewhere as well. People began craving it, as they used to crave money. Money became worthless. Some sort of energy inflation, one could say. Since the majority of people didn't know how to achieve such a state in a natural way, they started using some sort of implants that became increasingly popular.*

*The memory card,* thought Jessica. *It numbs your reason and separates your consciousness from your body. A very unpleasant experience, believe me. However, it is true that it makes your body smile all the time. And that the body somehow doesn't feel the need for change. It answers and works instead of you. Horrible.*

*But, as we've suspected, the incredible power was hiding in the satellite headquarters, where these cards were being controlled. Imagine having the power over the entire planet. You'd press the button and the entire world would act the way you ordered it. Such power can be extremely dangerous and we're on the verge of losing the planet…*

*The entire planet?*

*I presume that after today's initiation you already know that we're not alone in the universe,* continued Aaron. I remembered the white scaly beings and agreed.

*Since we, the people, have fallen into straightforward destruction, the Rulers and the Darkened have agreed to dismantle the planet,* explained Ravi. *There are places of refuge, planets for survivors. The Rulers will soon announce the official*

*date of dismantling. This is where you come in, Derek. Your ability to travel. Have the Rulers told you what you have been initiated into?* he asked me.

*No. The only thing I know is that I had different clothes and much younger body after the procedure.*

*Then I think you should meet somebody,* said Keisha. *There,* she pointed southwards.

A brown-haired girl was waiting for me in the green grass. She was looking towards me and waved at me to come closer. I looked at the others and bid them farewell. As I was walking towards her I picked up my pace, because I could feel I was going to get the answers I had been looking forward to for quite some time...

## XXXIII. THE STORY OF POWER

»HELLO, DEREK,« SHE SAID WHEN WE MET. »My name is Elizabeth. But everybody calls me by my other name. My nickname is Timeless.« I shook her hand.

»I have to tell you that we're pretty much alike. That's why I'm going to tell you a story I've told no one before…«

»Please,« I said with interest. I could sense that the girl standing in front of me was much older than she looked. And I could feel her extraordinary power.

»As one of the Rulers, I got the task to cleanse this planet,« she continued. »Like Ravi and Ina. But I've fallen much deeper than any one of us. My first birth was marked with learning that I wanted to turn over to the people around me. But I wasn't aware of the fact that the vibration of the human body was so heavy and so full of emotions. And so I soon started using the knowledge that I had in me since I came to this world for my own purposes. When I saw that people didn't want to follow the knowledge I had, I started exploiting it… I wanted fame and I got it. I wanted wealth and I got it. I wanted love and I got it by force. All of that was, of course, incompatible with the laws of nature. However, during that time the planet had much heavier magnetic field that enabled such abuse of power. People were completely intoxicated by my power. I could've had anything and anybody.«

Such a story seemed doomed in advance.

»And it was. During my reign I attracted the attention of beings called the Darkened. In this body I had a significantly lower soul vibration than

before, when I was one of the Rulers. In my greed for more power I surrendered to theirs. What happened was quite the opposite from what I
had expected: I was betrayed. They robbed me of my powers and plunged
me into the lowest sphere of existence in the universe. There any hope of
escape is almost nonexistent. I could say that I spent the whole eternity
there before it occurred to me how I could get out…«

»And how did you do it?« I asked.

»I realized that I had a lot of weaknesses in me. But where there is
a lot of weakness, there's also a lot of strength. I regretted my action so
deeply that, through special procedures, I discovered my ability that only
a few rare beings in the universe have.«

»And that is?«

»That is my nickname,« she smiled. »In my soul I found a frequency
of bridges that connect the universe. Some bridges or wormholes connect
great distances. The others connect *time*.«

I almost couldn't follow her explanation anymore.

»Time wormholes. I discovered when and in what way I needed to
connect with them. When I clearly stated my intention, time worked
for me. And because I really wanted to do good, my ability of traveling
through time improved to such accuracy that the Rulers – who welcomed
me back again – gave me the nickname Timeless. I went back to the time
before my reign and completely repaired all the damage I had caused to
the planet. Since then I've been known as one of the most just queens
in the world. But soon I felt the need to step back and the Rulers sensed
that too. We made a plan what the end of my existence should look like
and executed it. From then on I've been secretly moving among those
who truly want my knowledge. And sincerely want to help the planet.«

I was amazed by the incredible story I had just heard. The girl looked
familiar, that much was true. But it'd never occur to me that she had
such a rich history.

»And I can sense this resemblance in you,« she added. »There's a lot
of regret in you, because you did things you didn't really want to do.

However, regret isn't the right emotion – an all-conquering confidence in a bright future would've been much more appropriate. Do you believe in a bright future, Derek?«

»Yes.« I'd succeeded in training my mind to the point where I could offer that answer quickly and without thinking, even though I was hindered sometimes by the weight of my past. I was thinking about my father. And whether Chig Lan would still be alive if I hadn't…

»Those are all obsolete thoughts. Forget what you'd done in the past. I've killed thousands of people and had to face intense darkness before I could overcome the power of fate and change it…«

»Does that mean that – I can change fate?«

»With the power that you carry inside you, you can do much more than that,« she said bravely.

»But I'm afraid that you don't have much time left. That's why I have to tell you that you've been given quite a special body during today's initiation. The body that can be teleported and can travel through time. You have the power to attract wormholes of the universe, just like me. There's only one detail that's very important. Since laws of nature don't support such traveling anymore, it's more of an exception than the rule. Your body can stay in the past for one hour, not longer. The vibration of your cells is adapted to the vibration of present time and not the past. But since you wish to use your ability for a good purpose, such traveling will be made possible for you when you're ready.«

Again I was amazed. The surprises just wouldn't stop coming.

»You have to know that there are dangers on this way and you have to be aware of them. The planet called Skatur, although meant as a refuge for the inhabitants of the universe, represents a great danger for you. Because of the wish for absolute peace, anyone found in that area will first be taken to planet Kanter and have their memory deleted, and will only then be sent to planet Skatur. That mustn't happen to you – otherwise you won't be able to fulfill your mission. If somebody asks you if you remember anything, your answer should be no and your thoughts empty. You must've learned that here by now.« She looked me straight in the eyes.

»Do you want to save this planet?« she asked me.

I remembered the crazed mob and flinched. »Of course,« I answered.

»Then you have to write a book.«

I raised my eyebrows. That was the last thing I'd expect.

»A book?« I asked disbelievingly.

»Three, actually,« she corrected me.

»THREE books? They told me in Sector Two that…«

»Yes, that's true. That's living in the now. But you're traveling to the past. And this writing will completely differ from what it used to be…«

I didn't know what to say to her.

»Go to Ravi and Ina. And Keisha and Jesse. Together you'll find the right solution. And keep in mind that it's urgent. The dismantling of the planet is scheduled for tomorrow,« she calmly concluded. »Don't worry. When the right time comes you'll know what you have to do,« she added and then disappeared in the sunlight.

# XXXIV. THE DISINTEGRATION

WE WERE STANDING IN A CIRCLE. We knew that we had only one shot. Soon we received the last warning from the Rulers:

»Leave, or you won't just die. You'll disintegrate.«

We looked at each other.

»It's all right,« said Ravi and looked at me, »If necessary, you know what you have to do. Protect Zyna.«

»And Kairon,« added Keisha.

»And for now: continue.«

I was holding a USB flash drive in front of me. It was small, oval and barely noticeable. The two couples stepped closer. They raised their hands and sent the contents we talked about into the small device I was holding in my hand. Then I did the same. A bright beam of light came out of my left hand and into the flash drive. The light that directed itself like a precise laser towards the microscopically small circuit finally found the appropriate space and settled down in the device. The four of them sighed with relief.

»It's done,« I confirmed.

»You're right, it really is *done*!« I heard a hoarse voice behind my back. Without turning around I quickly swallowed the USB flash drive.

»Go now, Derek,« calmly said the blonde. »You're not on our side! There's no place among us for those who yielded to the darkness!« I thought that she could put more effort into dramatizing her words and I wasn't sure that the Darkened would believe her. Luckily I was wrong. I turned around and slowly walked towards the basement.

»You think you're done with us. Unfortunately... you've just begun!« said the hoarse voice. The dark beings scattered around the room and soon I couldn't see anything anymore. Luckily for me they initially left me alone. As we had expected. I closed the door behind me, but it soon started to crack. Horror-stricken I watched how precisely the plan was unfolding. It *really* was pre-arranged for the planet to disintegrate!

Mourning for my friends I ran quickly to save the last treasure I'd been entrusted with: the children.

Three prepared capsules were waiting in a scrap iron container. Zyna and Kairon were waiting for me in the two smaller ones.

»Quickly, there's no time for games,« I told them. I tightly fastened their seat belts and prepared their toys. If everything went well, they'd soon land on Skatur.

»Where are you going, uncle Derek and where's mom?« asked little Zyna. I'd have been too difficult to explain to her that her mom had been dead for a few minutes. »Everything's fine, kid,« I told her quickly, »you're going on a short trip...«

»Can I go too?« asked Kairon.

»You too, but you have to be completely quiet!« I whispered. I exerted my remaining strength to keep my facial muscles smiling, so the children wouldn't be too scared. There was a long and dangerous journey ahead of them anyway.

»You can talk through this,« I told them and pointed at the silver button on the control board. I entered the settings for the autopilot and safe landing.

»Are you ready?« I asked them quickly with the widest possible grin.

»Yeees,« they were thrilled. I had a hard time hiding the tears at the thought that I'd probably never see them again.

»Is everything all right, uncle Derek?« asked the sensitive little Zyna. *She got that from her mother*, I thought.

»Yes, it is. Something got in my eye. Listen now. You're going on a magical trip and you have to promise me something. When you land, the world will be full of fairy-tale beings of all sorts and colors. But you have to remember something: if anybody asks you where you're from, you have to say that you don't remember anything, all right? That's very important!«

»But uncle Derek…« protested little Kairon.

»If you don't do that, those beings will hide me so well that you'll never find me again,« I was trying to make the truth a little bit more fairy-tale-like. »You'd like to see me again, wouldn't you…?« I asked them.

»Of course, uncle,« said Zyna.

»Well, all right. Here it goes…« I kissed the kids and tried to close the main glass lids as playfully as possible.

»See you,« I waved at them. I placed both capsules on the takeoff platform and pressed the Start button.

*Hang on, kids, I really hope to see you again…* I thought as the tunnels opened up. They waved at me one last time and it looked like they were taking a ride on a small train in an amusement park. I waved back at them playfully and tried to dance a silly little dance to prolong their carefree childhood as long as possible. *They're barely four years old and they've already lost everything*, I thought. *Absolutely everything.*

The light of the wormhole engulfed them. They were gone in a flash.

*It's my turn now*, I thought.

I climbed into a slightly bigger capsule that had been prepared on the next takeoff platform. As I was closing the lid I noticed that dis-integration had already started in the basement and it was a matter of seconds before it would reach me… *At least the children got out in time*, I tried to console myself.

I didn't have much time left. As I pressed the Start button I noticed that the tunnel was only partially open. I was launched and the last thing I saw was horrifying: only half of the planet that was still trying to defy its destiny, was spinning around its axis, and yet it was already completely

surrounded by darkness…

The tunnel that brought me away from the planet vanished in an instant. Obviously the connection was no longer possible! My capsule stopped at the very beginning of my journey and automatically started emitting the S.O.S. signal.

*Damn*, I thought, *I'm not going to make it!*

Soon one of the ships from Skatur came to my rescue, but I knew that I wouldn't be taken there. I knew where I was going to end up. I knew what my fate was.

*Please, forgive me for my failed plan*, I took one last look towards the disappearing planet, looking in vain for my lost friends… Soon the other half of the globe evaporated into nothing too.

## XXXV. THE VERDICT

MY CAPSULE'S VIBRATION WAS PICKED UP BY ONE OF THE SPACESHIPS that had been swarming in Earth's vicinity. It neutralized my navigation equipment in an instant and attached me to it. Soon I received the instruction to open the hatch.

When I entered the much bigger ship I was brought before its commander. I saw beings I'd never seen before. Besides the larger, white and scaly Rulers that were rare on this ship, there were yellow reptiles that were prevailing, purple people that were narrower than the other beings, and very large green snakes.

The commander was a yellow reptile, a member of the majority.

»Welcome to the Skaturian patrol,« he said. »I wonder if you know by any chance where you are headed?«

A couple of purple beings came up to me and I could feel they were connecting to my thought vibration. I remembered Timeless' instructions. And I remembered the peace I felt when I fought the commission in Sector Two.

*No thoughts. No thoughts.*

»No, I don't know,« I said confused. The beings next to me nodded to the reptile.

»Do you know your name?«

*No thoughts.*

»No,« I said again with my head empty.

»He's obviously been on Kanter, which is very interesting. But why is his vessel here, in the Earth's region...?« he was talking to the purple beings next to me.

For a moment I thought of Earth, how I saw it disintegrate in front of my eyes and I completely forgot that the beings were still connected to my thought frequency.

»Kanter, Kanter,« they started answering.

Before I knew it, I was branded and given some sort of a bracelet. I was brought to the capsule that contained a large number of people, Earthlings. The capsule's vibration was too heavy for me to teleport. And even if I could do that, where would I go? Earth had been destroyed.

Using a quick wormhole we soon arrived on the planet Kanter. We took our clothes off and received our respective numbers that were fixed to our bracelets. The electrodes were fixed to the backs of our heads and they stuck to the scalp like a magnet. When we lay down in the yellow liquid I felt a slight throbbing sensation at the back of my head. The group leader said that we needed to relax... For the last time I thought about how sorry I was that my plan had failed. I was hoping that I'd remember at least some small detail when I woke up.

I purposely started repeating the phrase »USB flash drive« before I fell asleep. There had to be a way for me to fulfill my mission ...

As I was lying in the liquid the vibration of the electrode was becoming stronger and faster. I could feel the needle come out of it, penetrating deep into my brain. Even though it didn't hurt, the feeling was nevertheless very unusual. The warmth in my head blended with my repetition of the phrase »USB flash drive«, sounding a bit like the even skipping of a broken record player... In the yellow liquid that we were able to breathe, we didn't need oxygen. All the nutrients and the oxygen that our bodies required, were in that liquid. I was floating in it like in a womb and started to feel safe... And I kept repeating those omnipresent words...

*USB flash drive, USB flash drive...*

## XXXVI. WAKING UP

I FELT PRESSURE IN MY HEAD. Something pulled me out of the liquid. I wiped it off my face catching my breath – oxygen was thinner on the outside – and opened my eyes. A robot was standing in front of me and she was more than obviously in a great hurry. I wouldn't attribute such a behavior to a robot. A loud alarmed sounded.

Even before I managed to regain full consciousness she helped me get dry and dressed and put on a spacesuit. I was able to breathe again. I noticed a microphone in the helmet and realized she could hear me. I wanted to know who she was and what had actually happened…

»What happened?« I asked her.

»There's no time for explanations,« she said quickly. »Come with us if you want to live!«

Another robot was sitting on the second platform and he offered me his hand. I climbed on his platform and we drove off in a hurry.

We were leading the way, while she was driving right behind us. When we approached the exit that began closing rapidly, I closed my eyes. We managed to avoid hitting the door by a hair's breadth. The robot behind us wasn't so lucky. We heard a loud bang as she collided with the door and got torn into a thousand pieces. The robot driving our shining platform stopped the vehicle and cried out:

»Zyna!«

A girl that seemed familiar appeared behind me. She was sitting on the platform right behind me.

»She's all right, Kairon, she managed to disconnect herself. If we hurry towards home we might still save her,« she said quickly. »Go!«

The robot pointed his vehicle away from the planet and I noticed that we were approaching some sort of a passage. The tunnel sucked us in and suddenly we found ourselves in front of a violet planet that was shining in the beauty of its moons and a star.

The robot pointed his vehicle towards the planet's right continent. Soon we landed next to one of the round houses. I don't know why, but when we landed I thought of the phrase »USB flash drive«. I couldn't get it out of my head.

»First we'll take care of Zyna and then of your USB flash drive, all right?« said the brown-haired girl.

I thought it was funny how I didn't ask her anything and she already gave me an answer. We rang the doorbell and a large being with turquoise scales, tail extending to the ground and glittering excrescences all over its body answered the door. Such a being also seemed familiar, but I didn't know where from. I thought again of the USB flash drive. The brown-haired girl put on a hat.

»I'm sorry to have to tell you that your robot Naia was damaged beyond repair and that we had to dismantle her. You'll get a new one soon,« she said.

»What a pity, we've gotten used to her,« said the apparently female being. »And Zyna loved her too.«

»Just as a precaution, to make sure that she didn't catch any of the robot's vibrations – may we examine her?« asked the brown-haired girl.

»I don't know how that could happen, but… Please. She's upstairs. She's still asleep, you know.«

We went up the stairs. We opened the door and there was a young girl lying on the bed. The robot next to me ran to her and embraced her. »Zyna,« he whispered and gently touched her cheek.

The brown-haired girl closed the door.

»Kairon, control yourself, we don't want somebody to see you,« she said sternly.

»And you'll be of much greater assistance to us if you remember who you are,« she smiled to me. »After all, there's something left. If they'd erased everything, restoration of your memory would be nearly impossible. Maybe you're the one who saved us with your relentless repetition of the phrase »USB flash drive«!« she smiled.

»Come here and sit next to me.«

»And hurry up!« said the robot. »Her pulse is slowing down!«

»Calm down, Kairon!« she said and then looked at me. »Try to relax as much as you possibly can…«

I closed my eyes. I felt some sort of a thick substance wash over my body… Like every cell in my body was bathing in its own indigenous frequency. I could feel that I was getting back the vibration of the body I had before I arrived on the planet with the yellow liquid… I was struck by a flash of lightning that spread from the middle of my forehead over my entire body… *My name is Derek.* And then the other memories came… *Ching Lan… Ina, Ravi, Kairon, Zyna… Save the planet Earth – USB flash drive!*

Suddenly, everything became clear to me. I looked at Timeless and said with a smile:

»USB flash drive!«

»But before that we have to save Zyna, agreed?« said Timeless.

## XXXVII. EPILOGUE

WE WERE SITTING BY HER BED, HELPING HER. We could see her soul trying to connect to the body, but her thread was partially torn and she couldn't make the connection. I entered this vibration and, using the dense frequency I sent to the damaged part of the cord, mended the tear. Timeless and Kairon also contributed a lot of power and Zyna finally managed to make the connection. She merged with her body and jerked her eyes open. She started gasping for air like somebody who just came from beneath the surface of the water.

»Zyna!« called out Kairon, still in the body of a robot.

»Kairon! I thought I'd never see you again!« said Zyna and embraced him. They kissed and the sight of that was slightly unusual: a robot and a girl...

Timeless led me away from the bed and put her hand on my belly.

»I hope it's not too late,« she said. I could feel a slight tingling sensation in my stomach. I knew what she was looking for and I helped her. Soon she was holding the USB flash drive I swallowed all those years ago.

»Time to relax,« said Timeless.

»Kairon, you'll be our player,« she smiled. »We'll connect to your thought vibration.«

Kairon took the USB flash drive and inserted it into the back of his neck. The information that had been asleep on the flash drive for quite a few years, came to life in his head. The light expanded into a color movie that we all watched simultaneously. Data transfer took a few minutes. When the light hid back in the flash drive again we all sighed deeply.

»My father was a rock star,« slowly uttered Kairon.

»And my parents… what power,« said Zyna and her eyes filled with tears. »And how they loved me…«

»Now, now,« quickly said Timeless. »If we want to save them, we have to hurry. The wormhole will open in a few minutes.«

»Derek,« said Zyna. »Maybe there is a reason why you had to come here.«

»What do you mean by that?« I asked her.

»Give me the flash drive,« she said with determination. In the silence of the room Kairon handed her the flash drive.

Zyna was holding the flash drive in front of her and it was obvious that she was filling it with love that only an exceptionally pure human being could possess.

»Mom, dad, this is for *you*,« she said quietly. She closed her eyes and suddenly the room was full of light. The entire room was bathing in the colors of the rainbow that were whirling around her bed. Soon the flash drive that Zyna was holding in front of her started pulling the colors in. When the light and the contents of her story ended up in the circuit, I managed to grasp the perfection of the universe's plan. I was meant to come here. To get to know Zyna and to hear her part of the story. There were no coincidences.

She handed me the USB flash drive.

»There you go, it's ready now. Have a safe journey, Derek. A *really* safe journey,« she said and hugged me. I felt the exceptional power of her love.

*I'll make it, Zyna – for your sake if nothing else,* I thought as Timeless and me rushed towards the house's front door.

I sat on the shining platform and brought it up in the air.

»There, you see?« she pointed with her finger.

I spotted a colorful tunnel.

*Don't forget, one hour,* she reminded me. *The year 2011.*

I was caught in a whirlwind repeating my demand in my head: *2011, 2011, 2011.*

The whirling suddenly stopped and I flew into the water. There were people around me and I realized that I ended up in a river. People were sitting on both banks of the river. I quickly got out of the water and tried to draw as little attention to myself as possible. My platform got stuck under a nicely decorated white bridge.

I took a look around me. I quickly climbed the well arranged concrete bank and tried to remember where my platform was.

»Excuse me, where am I?« I asked the first girl I saw who sitting on a concrete step.

She looked at me like that was something self-evident and answered in fluent English. »In Ljubljana. In Slovenia.«

»Oh, thank you so much,« I said. *That is excellent, nobody is going to bother me here.* I noticed that people in this place and time weren't infected with memory cards yet, which made me very happy.

I came to a square that was paved with small cubes. At one end there was a large statue of a man holding a book. Since I knew I only had an hour at my disposal, I quickly went up the first street I saw – it led upwards.

The residents of the city I stopped along the way directed me towards the nearest library. I asked to use a computer with the Internet access. I sat down and looked at my watch: I had forty-five minutes left.

I inserted my USB flash drive into the computer and started working. I was in luck, because the computer was – for its time – pretty powerful. I made up a female pseudonym and three book titles: The Frequency, Floodlight and Skatur. It took me fifteen minutes to set up a website.

*This has got to work, it just has to,* I thought as I was adding the »Buy« button. When I activated the website I had five minutes left to return to the bridge.

When I returned, my platform was still under the bridge.

*Where do I go now?* I thought. *I'll stay on this planet, no matter what,* I decided. *Even if that means dying with everybody else.*

I was driving along the river until I found a spot isolated enough that nobody would be able to witness my take-off. A rainbow-colored tunnel entrance was already waiting for me in the sky.

*Australia, the year 2021*, I thought. *City of Happiness. 2021.*

I purposely chose the year after the disintegration of the world. I kept repeating the demand in my head until I felt a hard bump against the soft green surface...

»Are you all right?« I heard a familiar voice ask. A pair of dark eyes filled with love was looking at me.

»What kind of question is that?« I was surprised to see her again. »You better tell me if *you* are all right?« I replied. »I only recently found out that you're...«

»That I'm what? Here?« she said and pointed around herself. The bright green grass full of colorful flowers stood out from the rest of the surroundings. I was lying in the green softness, marveling at the round-shaped architecture around me. Quite a few domes were glittering around us and it seemed that they were some sort of buildings.

»Do you like it here?« she asked pointing around.

»Very much,« I replied. It seemed that both of us still knew we belonged together, even if this time everything was coming along entirely differently... We heard a call and turned around. Only then I noticed that I was lying on a bluish-green platform. Keisha and a dark-haired boy ran up to us. They both looked beautiful, yet slightly worried.

»Derek! Are you all right?« she asked me. The boy took a step towards me and it struck me that we looked alike.

Keisha stopped him with her hand. "Wait, Jim. Let him get used to it."

*Why does everybody keep asking me that? Yes, I'm all right*, I thought.

I quickly stood up to clear my head. I took a look around and realized that City of Happiness as I knew it no longer existed. The top of the plateau I was standing on was offering a magnificent outlook: beautiful forests that separated vast estates were full of smiling people whose abilities and youth reminded me of the people in Sector One. Only now the social classes were gone. What used to separate people indicating their

level of development was now making them different merely in view of their abilities. The awareness of happiness, the abilities once considered supernatural and the wisdom once granted only to few were now at the disposal of every single inhabitant of the planet. The children were playing in the sun; some were moving or creating objects by the sheer power of thought, some flying around with butterflies, some sending pockets of light energy to the plants. The birds were greeting each and every part of this green creation. The animals surrounding the people seemed like conscious creators' happy helpers. The people were creating and rejoicing. Everything was simply wonderful.

My love stood up as well and took my face in her hands.

»Congratulations, Derek,« she said. She brought her lips to mine and welcomed me in the new reality.

## ACKNOWLEDGMENTS

I thank my husband and agent Jan Sebastian Srečkar, who was the first to read and comment on my work the entire time of the writing. He has also helped me with some wonderful ideas that I used in this book. I am also grateful for his emotional support which I will never forget.

I thank my mom for a true example of mother's unconditional love. Without her help and unshakable faith it would have been much harder for me to realize my goals and my vision.

I thank my family: my father Zvone and sisters Mojca and Špelca for additional energy, their views about my work and their support. I also thank Ivan Sečkar and Metka Zadravec, my friends Benko and Sara Mrđanović, and also my programmer Edis Talunđić for his dedicated collaboration and patience.

For their infinite patience, help and support I thank the translators Mojca Lorber and Alan Horvatić. Their work is truly great and precious. I am also very grateful to Pia Rihtarič, the designer of the wonderful pictures and ornaments for this trilogy and Katja Pirc for graphical design.

My thanks go to those who have built the life as I know it with their inspiring knowledge: Polona Sepe, Slavko Mahne-Shyama, Foster Perry, Luna, Matej Škufca, Eros with his book [psi], Rhonda Byrne with The Secret and Vladimir Megre with his book collection Anastasia.

I also thank all those that have read the trilogy and thus became a part of our shared adventure.

# ABOUT THE AUTHOR

Janja Srečkar is a versatile artist (author, poet, director, actress, dancer, singer; a music teacher by profession) and a fan of science-fiction literature. She is especially drawn to the protagonists with special powers. She has a wide array of favorite authors and their main quality is that they strengthen the message they wish to convey with the use of love and humor. Among her favorite authors are Vladimir Megre, Eros, Charlotte Bronte, Gustav Šilih, Bogdan Novak, Richard Bach, Stephen Turoff, Paramhansa Yogananda, Shirley Maclaine, Rhonda Byrne and Stephenie Meyer. In author's own words her mission is "to mask" positive messages - that benefit our everyday life as well as our future - into packages of art (printed publications, theatrical performances, poems...) that people accept, understand and possibly even have fun with."

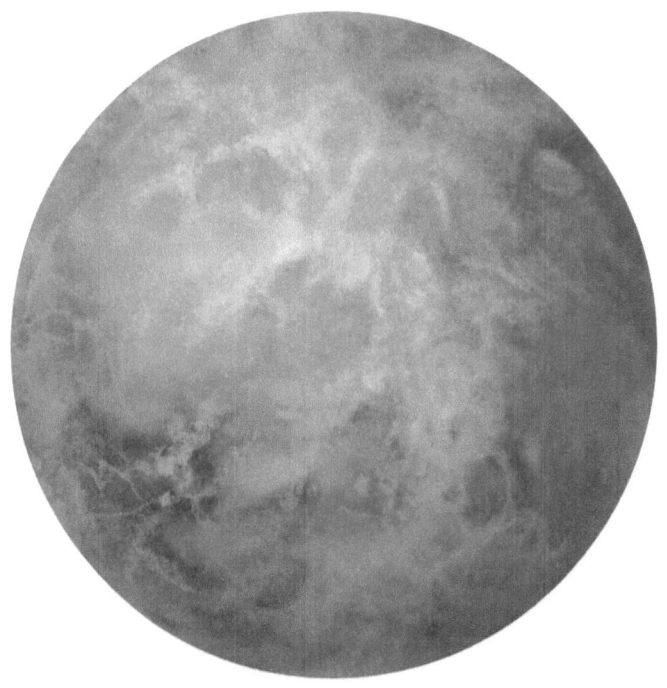